MURDER AT LOLLY BEACH

— AN EVE SAWYER MYSTERY —

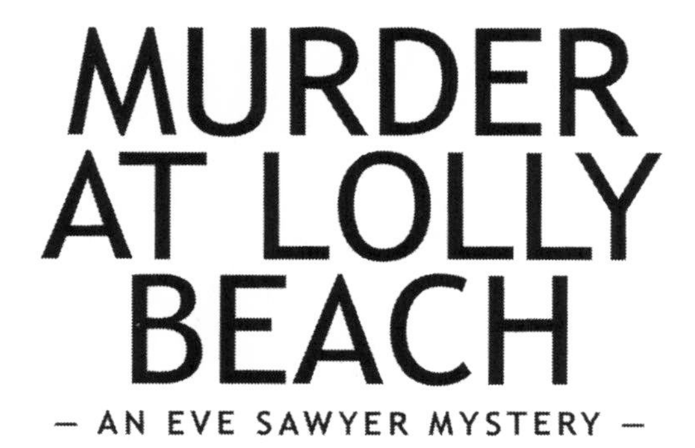

JANE SUEN

Murder at Lolly Beach: An Eve Sawyer Mystery

Copyright © 2021 by Jane Suen

All rights reserved.

No part of this book may be reproduced in any form or by any electronic, mechanical, photocopying, or other means including information storage and retrieval systems, without prior written permission from the author. The only exception is for a reviewer who may quote short excerpts from the book in a review. Thank you for your support of the author's rights.

This book is a work of fiction. Names, characters, places, and incidents are products of the author's imagination or are used fictitiously. Any resemblance to actual persons, living or dead, events, or locales is coincidental.

Jane Suen books are available for order through Ingram Press Catalogues.

www.janesuen.com

Printed in the United States of America

First Printing: January 2021

Library of Congress Control Number: 2020924750

Ebook ISBN: 978-1-951002-14-5

Paperback ISBN: 978-1-951002-15-2

Audiobook ISBN: 978-1-951002-16-9

For a better future for our oceans and the animals who share our planet.

AUTHOR'S NOTE

Inspired by the best crêpes I've ever had—and could never find again since that one sweltering summer on a beach in South Carolina—this book is a work of fiction.

PROLOGUE

He whistled. Next to him on the passenger seat sat a basket of fresh, ripe peaches, their aroma wafting through the cabin of the truck. Not just any peaches, though. The first in-season Georgia peaches. It was still too early for South Carolina peaches. Blake had rushed to close shop and drive across the border to a local farm with a fruit stand, which remained open until dark. The peaches had looked divine, and a quick bite confirmed the sweet, juicy fruit was worth the trip. Tomorrow, he'd make his magic. His shiny blade would be ready to cut through the fuzzy skin, parting it to expose the ripe fruit.

Blake checked the clock on the dashboard—9:32 p.m. It was dark already; the coolness of the evening had descended. He passed the bridge and the sign for Lolly Beach, traveling down the single main street, central to the small beach town. At the light, he turned left, then a sharp right into a food truck parking lot. He parked his pickup and turned off the engine before dashing inside his food truck with the freshly picked peaches.

Blake didn't hear the click of the doorknob. Facing the counter, his back was turned, intent on making sure everything was ready for the big day tomorrow. Blake shivered as a thrill of excitement tingled up his spine.

His fingers caressed the soft fuzz of the peach and traced the round curve, going down the seam until it reached the tip, ending at the sharp point.

❧

THEY HAD MET under the moonlight. On the beach. The wind had stirred the water, and the salty spray mixed with the moisture-laden air embraced them. They raced to the ocean and felt the icy sting of the water slap against their legs. Powerful waves surged inland, losing steam after crashing on the beach and frothing into the sand. The waves chased them back. They ran, out of breath. The moonbeams softened her face, betraying the childlike adoration in her eyes. Her lips parted. He felt the pressure of her warm lips, then the grip of her arms wrapped around his body, straining to close the gap. His feeble protests lost to the wind, dispersed by sea breezes. Powerful waves surged, swell after swell, relentless, urgent, slapping the shore. Primal desires overwhelmed his senses, rising as their joint cries reached a crescendo.

❧

BLAKE DIDN'T HEAR the footsteps of the man who had crept up behind him. He didn't see the man raise his arm.

The thump was the last sound as his body hit the floor. The man silently retreated out the way he came. Inside, a solitary peach rolled out of Blake's unclenched hand and made its way across the floor toward the open door.

CHAPTER ONE

EARLIER IN THE DAY

I DIDN'T NEED THE ROAD SIGN TO TELL ME I WAS getting closer to the ocean, but my heart pounded when the first unmistakable one appeared. Palm trees dotted the landscape and lined the road. The sun blazed overhead. I rolled down the window to take a deep inhale, catching a gust of sea wind as it swept into my ratty, old car. I licked my lips, expecting a slight salty taste as I propelled forward, my foot pressing down on the gas pedal, leaving puffs of smoke trailing from my tailpipe as I approached the beach.

A switch clicked in my mind, shutting out all thoughts of Midway College. An involuntary smile crossed my lips. The crazy end of the semester was over. I had finished writing my term paper on Murder Creek and the missing Lacey Walken, and turned it in to Professor Reynolds. I cleared out a few things left on my plate and paid my bills before I left town. Done with classes and exams, I wanted to have fun at the beach. Sunbathe. Read books. Frolic in the ocean. Watch the sunset. Hang out at the oyster bar. Squish hot, burning sand under my feet and between my slender toes. I didn't have a worry in the world. I felt as free as the wind twirling and teasing strands of my hair, whipping it across my face.

Cassie, my lab mate at college, had invited me to spend some time with her at the beach, staying at her family's charming, quaint cottage. A change of scenery was what I needed. I could see myself lounging in a comfy chair or lying on a colorful towel spread on the sand as the waves crashed. Or kicking off my shoes and running toward the ocean, joining the swimmers, their heads bobbing in the water, as the pulsating rhythm of the waves beckoned, drawing me closer to its vastness, beauty, and power.

Her invite came at a good time. More than good—it was great. Perfect timing. I felt exhilarated, looking forward to some well-earned R & R, lazy days of doing nothing, or whatever I felt like. I couldn't wait to hang out with Cassie. I'd met her in chemistry this semester. We ended up in lab together—Bob, too. It was a tough class, and together, we plowed through it and became fast friends before semester's end. What a trio we were —Cassie, the striking, leggy redhead; Bob, lanky and serious, with unruly hair; and me, slim-framed, with thick, tawny hair.

We had worked out an agreement for the stay. In return for the free rent, I would buy the groceries, and Bob would contribute to the expenses and buy other items as needed. We'd both help with the chores. Cassie and I would take turns cooking when we didn't go out to eat.

❧

MUSIC BLARED from the car stereo. Long, slender legs thrust out of the open window on the driver's side, toenails painted a brash sea-blue color, with strings of hemp anklets dangling around slim ankles. I smiled, pulling into the narrow parking space behind her car parked in the driveway.

Oh yeah, it was Cassie all right. Independent, spirited, sexy. She had to take a required science course, and struggled in class. If it weren't for my help, she wouldn't have made it through. Cassie had tried her hardest and was proud of earning a C-minus. The class, though, ended any inclination of pursuing the medical career her father had insisted on when he paid for her college tuition. If she stayed in pre-med, she would've had to take biochemistry the next semester. It was common knowledge how much harder the advanced class would be, and with it, a slimmer chance of Cassie getting a passing grade. No way she was going to take it. It took a great deal of cajoling, mixed with tears and pleading, to placate her miffed, angry father and convince him she didn't want to become a doctor. Would his conscience be clear if she blundered her way through medical school and misdiagnosed patients? Dear old Dad finally got the message.

Cassie's heart was in the arts. Her good-faith

attempts in taking the chemistry class helped to smooth over her father's protests, and cranking up her charm as Daddy's little girl didn't hurt. Even her grandmother, Nora, had chimed in on Cassie's behalf, saying the girl may have inherited her creative genes. Nora had been a patron of the arts, and she dabbled in painting herself. This artsy beach house was her grandmother's.

I hopped out of my car, slammed the door, and looked inside Cassie's window. She had her eyes closed. "Cassie," I called out softly. When she didn't respond, I tapped on the car.

CHAPTER TWO

SHE STIRRED, OPENING ONE EYE AND THEN THE OTHER. Cassie flicked the thick curls of her flaming red hair behind her ears and flashed a smile, pulling her legs back in. She jumped out of the car to greet me.

"Eve! You're here."

We hugged, acting like excited little girls, giggling and laughing. This change in scenery had changed my mindset and brought out the child in me, playing in the sand long ago. I still remembered the gaudy swimsuit I wore, the gritty sand slipping inside the fabric and sticking to my butt and in-between. I'd worn a floppy pink hat my mother had bought to protect my delicate baby skin from the sun. She'd smoothed suntan lotion on my face and everywhere.

"I made fresh lemonade," Cassie said, reaching for my one piece of luggage. "C'mon in. I'll show you to your room."

I followed, stepping over the threshold as the screen door snapped shut. A blast of cool air greeted me. The bright interior of the cottage was breathtaking—painted in a beautiful shade of sea-blue and tastefully decorated in a vibrant beach motif. An assortment of seashells and colorful glass bottles lined the white counter separating the living room from the kitchen. Pastel blue-green mugs and matching plates and bowls were displayed on shelves behind the glass doors of the kitchen cabinets. Above the comfy white couch, fish netting was artfully strung on the living room wall, with small seashells and crabs intertwined between the strands. It took me into Neptune's world.

"It's so cute," I mumbled. "Who decorated this?"

"Nora, and I helped her."

I stood there, admiring the décor.

"Would you like to see your room?" Cassie asked. She led the way to the first door on the right in the hallway. I glimpsed a double bed. Wallpaper with sail-boats plastered the walls instead of paint. A seashell mirror hung above the white distressed-wood dresser.

I scurried over to the bed and plopped on the pastel-blue woven cover, claiming it.

"I hope you don't mind sharing it." Cassie said.

"Oh," I said, barely keeping the disappointment out of my voice. I wanted this cute, bright, nautical room to myself.

Cassie laughed, pointing to the bedroom across the hall. "I'm in there."

"Where's Bob going to sleep?"

"There's a closet-sized room down the hall barely big enough to hold a twin-sized bed." Cassie chuckled.

"He can sleep there or crash on the couch. I'll give him a choice when he comes."

A twinge of guilt flashed as I thought of Bob relegated to the closet while I luxuriated in a room to myself. "When's he coming?" I quickly asked.

"Tomorrow. Why don't you get settled in first?" Cassie said.

CHAPTER THREE

I QUICKLY UNPACKED BEFORE JOINING CASSIE IN THE kitchen. She had poured two tall glasses of lemonade and waited for me. I swirled my drink, clinking the ice cubes. Beads of water rolled down the slippery glass, moistening my fingertips. I chugged the chilled liquid, taking long, satisfying gulps. The tang of fresh lemons awoke my taste buds, igniting a delightful burst of flavor, bitter-tangy sweetness mixed in pieces of fleshy pulp.

"Oh, this is delicious." I smacked my lips, flicking my tongue to catch a few drops perched on the rim of the glass.

"You had a good trip?"

I nodded and leaned back against the kitchen counter. "I took my time driving down."

"I'm glad you came," Cassie said.

"Sure, thanks for inviting me."

"No problem. I wasn't sure when you'd get away."

"It all worked out," I said, as my thoughts briefly

flickered to Murder Creek. I smoothed my hair and tucked a strand behind my ear.

Cassie laughed. "Now, we're going to relax and have some fun!"

"Yeah," I cheered, raising my near-empty glass of lemonade. "I can't wait."

Miles away, my old college world was far off and forgotten. This change in scenery was exactly what I needed. I didn't get away for spring break and got teased plenty for it. My mind needed a break. My body had muscles wound so tight it was all knots. Yup, I was ready for lazy days on the beach—listening to the soothing sound of ocean waves, watching Jet Skis and colorful boats sail by or planes flying overhead with banners. Days when time didn't matter, glued to a beach chair under a giant umbrella, reading books or falling asleep sunbathing. Medicine for the mind, body, and soul.

"We can go lay on the beach," Cassie said.

"You got chairs and umbrellas?"

"In the hall closet. After we use them, we can leave them outside. There's an outdoor faucet and hose to rinse the sand off."

I threw a bottle of sunscreen, a towel, flip-flops, and a worn-out hat in my beach bag and changed quickly into my bathing suit. Sunglasses were perched on my head.

I rushed out into the bright sunlight.

CHAPTER FOUR

We found a perfect spot on the sand to pitch our umbrellas. I slipped out of my flip-flops and wiggled my manicured toes as I stretched out on the beach chair, one hand limply hanging over the edge.

Above, the sky was solid blue, intense and clear, without a cloud or puff of wind. Directly ahead, the ocean stretched and flowed as far as I could see. I relaxed to the rhythmic sound of waves crashing gently on the sand and retreating as they left a layer of foam behind. It was idyllic, peaceful. I could stay put and not move at all. I surrendered to all the laziness I could muster without feeling a bit of guilt.

"I've missed this," Cassie said, brushing sand from her toned legs.

She looked great in a swimsuit. A thick, leonine mane of lush red locks framed an oval face. Lithe and slim, her moves were natural, feminine, yet not bashful. She had a natural grace. I remembered her long, slender fingers molding a piece of clay, shaping it to an object of beauty. She had a knack for art. Cassie had the talent. It was in her blood.

I'd been to the white, sandy beaches and the placid, crystal-clear, emerald-blue waters of the Gulf. Here, now, I was drawn to the brown-tinged sand and the powerful waves of the Atlantic Ocean as it churned, muddying the water until you couldn't see the bottom clearly, as it pulled and stirred up something inside me. Dark and real, to the edge of danger.

A shirtless guy chose this moment to cross our line of sight. His upper body gleamed, tanned and muscular.

Cassie took off her oversized sunglasses and turned to me, her lips pouting.

I laughed and shook my head. "You thinking what I'm thinking?"

"Tall, broad shoulders, and handsome."

"Hey, what about the guy … you know, in our chemistry class?"

Cassie shrugged and plopped her sunglasses back on.

She attracted men like moths to a flame. In the time I'd known Cassie, she dated guys—well, frankly, a lot of guys. But she was straightforward and didn't lead them on. She'd had mini crushes lasting as quick as a millisecond. But I'd never seen Cassie lose her heart over them.

We were quiet for a while. I felt the sweat rolling down my neck, finding its way to my chest and trickling between my breasts toward my belly button.

"Grandma Nora hasn't been well," Cassie said. She

had flipped over, stretched out and prone, her head facing me. "She's always been strong, healthy, and active. Lately, Nora's having trouble walking, and her strength is ebbing. I'm afraid she's having a hard time."

"Oh, no."

"I'll see her later today." She paused. "Would you like to meet her? She lives a few miles farther inland."

Cassie had talked about Nora, and I knew they had a special bond. Something beyond blood and kinship. I was curious about this woman Cassie adored, whose beach house we were living in. I wanted to meet her.

"I'd love to," I said.

CHAPTER FIVE

NORA WASN'T WHAT I HAD PICTURED—A FEEBLE, WHITE-haired lady. She was reclined on a porch swing when we arrived, a stunning picture of grace and fading beauty. A colorful shawl was thrown over the back of the swing. Even in a relaxed pose, she exuded dignity. Her beautiful locks, once her crowning glory from old photos I'd seen, was a limper, thinner version of her once-full head of hair.

Cassie had a tendency to overexaggerate. Her free-spirited nature embellished on occasion. It only added to my curiosity of Nora. Close up, I could see the lines carved on her face. Raw and unpretentious, it was a natural canvas untouched by a surgeon's scalpel. I knew I'd like her even before we exchanged words. I smiled.

A gentle breeze stirred, blowing the sheer porch curtain. Bright sunlight streamed through the flimsy white fabric, landing on the painted floor. Somewhere, wind chimes tinkled, chiming in chorus, uttering a melodic string of notes.

"Nora." Cassie hugged and kissed her. A pleased nod and peck on the cheek was the response she got.

"My dear, who did you bring?" Nora said, eyeing me as I stood quietly.

"Eve, my best friend from college." Cassie gestured to me. "We met when we became lab partners."

Nora smiled invitingly. The warm spark in her eyes was unmistakable.

"Pleased to meet you, ma'am," I murmured, pushing back an urge to do a curtsy.

"No formalities here." She glanced at Cassie and back to me. A half-smile tugged her lips. "Call me Nora ... Everyone else does."

Waving her arm toward a set of cushioned rattan chairs, Nora said, "Please, have a seat."

A pitcher of iced tea sat on a small, round table. Cassie brought out two empty glasses and sat them next to Nora's half-full drink.

"Help yourself," Nora said as she slipped out a fan and flicked it open.

I poured two glasses and handed one to Cassie. I sipped the iced tea, the cool fluid wetting my parched lips.

"How was your trip?" Nora asked.

I felt Nora's eyes on me before I caught her gaze and her lips moving, asking the question.

I shook my head. "Sorry, I was daydreaming about the beach. So different from the mountains I left a few short hours ago." I paused to set my glass down, looking for a coaster.

She pushed a napkin my way. "Don't worry about it. It ages the wood." Sure enough, dark rings had left their marks on the table top. Moisture had seeped in the cracks and warped the smooth texture. Yet the patterns created a mystique for me. I wondered who had sat on the porch with Nora and clinked ice cubes in glasses, sipping the cold beverage. Were they old friends from long ago? Lovers?

My active imagination pictured Nora in her youthful prime, surrounded by admirers. She was breathtaking, and she knew it—and the men knew it. She juggled her time, giving a glance to one while talking to another with a flirtatious air. Somehow, Nora conveyed she had all the time in the world, and each man felt her attentions were on him, and him alone. She held court with her admirers. The world was her oyster.

And what of Nora now—would she still recall them, their names and faces? I sensed she had many men, yet she guarded her heart. A scene flashed. A garden party. An opulent lifestyle. The women in their soft pastel dresses, the men in white semi-formal attire. Murmured conversations. The wind playing with soft tresses, teasing and freeing a few strands from carefully done coiffures. Sudden, full-throated laughter turning heads. Pairs of icy female eyes following the sound, targeting Nora, throwing darts of scorn and jealousy.

Nora was having the time of her life and didn't pay attention to their looks. She had her revenge, or rather took it, as boyfriends and husbands alike swarmed to her side, giving her a choice of playthings. At the height of her beauty, she had her pick. But as the years went by and looks faded, Nora shriveled in size and stature. I sensed her heart still beat strong. She was a tough old woman.

❧

CASSIE WAS CHATTING to Nora now about her classes. She gestured toward me when my name came into the conversation. She filled Nora in about us, and about me, my extrasensory perceptions, and the cold case I solved at Murder Creek.

"So that's how you met," Nora said, settling back in the chair. Her eyelashes fluttered as her lids closed.

"We've tired you," Cassie said. She gently pulled Nora up. "Let me help you inside."

Nora didn't protest. Cassie waved me off as she supported Nora, guiding her into the house.

CHAPTER SIX

We traveled on a bumpy road headed toward town from Nora's place. I could feel the loose gravel and the bumps and turns. Once we were near town, the road was paved. Cassie and I did some quick errands. She stopped at the store, and I picked up some supplies and toiletries. Then we drove to the corner grocery store to stock up for the next few days. We did pretty well finding what we wanted, as we had discussed it beforehand. I had told Cassie that I don't eat meat, but I will eat seafood on occasion. We planned to go out a few nights to sample the fresh seafood and the local cooking. I knew what I could manage on my student budget, and I'd told Cassie I wanted the money to stretch over the summer, before my federal student loan, grant money, and small stipend arrived in the fall.

We loaded our groceries and headed back. It didn't take long to prepare a simple meal of mixed salad greens and tart, zinging pesto pasta with olive oil, slivered almonds, baby spinach, cilantro, garlic, and a sprinkling of fresh lemon juice. The food was delicious, and I'd prepared the right amount for the two of us. We did the dishes together when we were finished eating. By then, I was looking forward to resting and sinking my head down on the soft, fluffy pillow.

"What time tomorrow?" I asked.

Cassie winked. "I'll let you sleep in. But if it's past nine, I'll come knocking on your door."

CHAPTER SEVEN

My eyes flickered open. It took me a minute to place where I was. The framed watercolor hanging on the wall of a woman wearing a huge beach hat triggered my memory. I stretched, smiling, as I rustled the smooth, soft cotton sheets. I didn't set an alarm. But boy, did I sleep well. The bed wasn't too bad, either. The mattress had the right amount of firmness, not too soft or saggy. I turned to check the time on my phone, snatching it off the nightstand. It was early, about half-past seven.

I quickly dressed and left the room to start the day. I was on the hunt for coffee.

Cassie was already in the kitchen. "Coffee?" she asked.

I nodded. We were going to get along just fine. "What's the brew?"

She picked up the package. "A dark roast from Guatemala ... rich, bold flavor and smooth taste."

"Perfect," I said.

She grabbed two mugs from the cabinet, poured the coffee, and set them on the kitchen table before taking a seat beside me.

"What's the plan for today?" I asked.

A silly grin spread over her face. I could read Cassie like a book. Like a child bursting with a secret and waiting for someone to ask so she could tell. Her eyes gleamed with the excitement.

"You gonna tell me or what?" I blurted out.

"I'm taking you to the best breakfast place in town," Cassie said.

"Where is it?"

"It's near Central Avenue, in a large parking lot."

I was intrigued. What was she talking about? "Wait, you're not taking me to a restaurant?"

"No, ma'am. I'm taking you to the food-truck stop."

I laughed. Breakfast at a foodie truck would be a first for me. "What do they serve?"

"Crêpes," she said, gesturing grandly. "All kinds. Eggs and cheese, ham, sausage, vegetarian, smoked salmon, cream cheese, and fruit. He makes them fresh and serves them wrapped as a cone."

My interest was raised, and my belly grumbled as if on cue. I'd be fine with vegetarian crêpes. What else was Cassie going to surprise me with?

"Today's special is peaches and crème crêpes. Ta-da!" Cassie announced. "He told me he was picking up fresh, sweet peaches straight from a Georgia farm."

I downed the last of my coffee. "He who?"

Cassie's cheeks flushed crimson red. "Blake," she murmured.

My stomach let out another growl as I got up. Since I wasn't getting details from Cassie now, I might as well go see this Blake for myself. "Let's go."

"My treat," she said, giving me a wink.

CHAPTER EIGHT

By now, I had a rough idea of the lay of the land. Central Avenue ran straight through the middle of the town. Restaurants, bars, clothing stores, and beach shops filled the real estate on both sides of the road. On the side streets were some older establishments, like the grocery store we'd shopped at. Cassie drove down one of the tree-lined side streets toward the center of town, turning left into a parking lot with food trucks. Fluttering yellow tape caught my eye, stretched across the front of a truck.

Cassie stomped her foot on the brake and screeched to a stop. She sucked in her breath. I glanced at her. It wasn't only the look on her ashen face or the way her fingers gripped tightly around the wheel. It was a disruption to the peaceful mood and the bright start of the morning. I had a sinking feeling. I followed her gaze to a group of people gathered in front of a food truck. She sat there and stared, searching the crowd. I wondered if she was hoping to see someone she knew. When Cassie's shoulders slumped, I knew she'd failed.

"You okay?" I asked.

She shook her head. "Something's happened to Blake."

I glanced at the crêpe food truck, the back door cracked halfway open, and wondered if he was inside. It was dark, and I couldn't see much. The yellow tape draped across the entrance and the police officers partially obscured my view.

Cassie gripped the car door handle, her body stuck to the seat. I opened my door and hopped out, stepping around to the other side to help. I had never seen Cassie like this. I feared for the worst. I didn't even know this guy Blake, the one who made the crêpes she'd been raving about. I needed to find out what was happening or talk Cassie into coming back later. Had something bad happened to Blake?

"I'm sorry," I blurted out. "Why don't you stay in the car, and I'll go check it out?"

A sigh escaped her trembling lips.

I squeezed Cassie's arm. I didn't know what else to say or how to reassure her. Maybe it was because I needed to be reassured myself. The yellow tape and police presence made the crime scene all too real.

CHAPTER NINE

USUALLY, CASSIE PARTED WAVES WHEN SHE APPROACHED a group. They'd open up and crowd around her. This time, it was different. She was outside, watching the crowd, as if an invisible line held her back. It was as though Cassie didn't belong.

I nudged my way into the crowd, my shoulder bumping into a tall, slender woman wearing beat-up jeans and a sheer cotton shirt, hair tied in a ponytail.

"Excuse me," I said.

She turned sideways, her dark brown eyes probing.

"You know him?" I asked, giving an apologetic smile.

She nodded. "And you?"

"No, but my friend does," I said, gesturing in Cassie's direction. "What's going on?" I stretched my neck, craning for a better view.

"I came to get my morning coffee and breakfast," she said.

I turned and moved closer, determined not to miss a single word.

A high-pitched laughter blasted in my ear. "Well, I'd overslept and was in a foul mood. I scrambled to get dressed and made a mad dash here. Blake makes his coffee badass and strong, the way I like it." She paused, giving me a stern look. "You know?"

I shook my head slowly from side to side. "No, this is my first time here."

"If you've had his crêpes, you'd know why they're out of this world. The first time, I passed on it—I didn't want a crêpe for breakfast. But once I tried one, I had to have more. He has several varieties. Blake mentioned he'd have something special today."

"What?"

"He wouldn't say. He only said it was special." The last few words caught in her throat. "I was pissed when I woke up late," she said, repeating this as if to admonish herself.

"Did you see him?"

She shook her head. "When I got here, it was too late."

"Oh, no," I said, my mouth falling open. *Too late, meaning he's dead?*

"The ambulance ..."

"Is he still alive?" I stuttered, as a flutter quickened my heartbeat.

"They're taking him to the hospital across the bridge. It's the nearest one."

I sighed in relief. I hadn't met the man, didn't know him, but still.

"When did you get here?" I asked.

"A few minutes before eight, when he opens."

"Were you the first?"

"No, a line had already started forming. You know, to get his special and all. Anyway, we waited past eight. I thought he needed the time to work, to get the special ready for us." She shook her head. "It was strange. Quiet. I worried something was wrong when he didn't open up the window to take our orders after more time had passed. Some people started calling out his name. When there was no answer, a guy at the front of the line poked his head inside the rear door."

"Who?" I asked.

She pointed to a guy wearing a neon orange T-shirt.

"Did he talk to the police?"

"Yup, earlier."

"Did he go in the truck?"

"Briefly. I heard he didn't want to mess up the crime scene, after seeing how they do it on TV."

"Any other customers go in?"

"No." She paused. "How did you hear about this place?"

"My friend Cassie," I said. "She's been gushing about his crêpes. Said I had to try them. Said he was making a special crêpe today. She was all excited about it."

"Your friend's not looking too good."

I glanced at Cassie. She was anything but excited. She looked deflated, like the air had been let out of a balloon.

"Listen, I gotta go. I'm Eve, by the way. Nice meeting you ...?"

"Kaitlyn," she said.

I left, hurried over to Cassie, and explained what I'd learned. When I mentioned the hospital, a spark flashed in her dull eyes.

CHAPTER TEN

We went back to the beach house. I was useless until I had food in my belly, and I insisted on making Cassie breakfast. I figured she could use another cup of coffee, too. She wasn't hungry, she said at first. I put generous pats of butter in the pan and fried two eggs, one for each of us. While they sizzled in the skillet, I set the table.

When the eggs were done cooking, I brought them over. She stared at her plate, the fried egg plopped in the middle, a buttery stream sliding down the medium-cooked yolk, leaving a dark yellow streak. It was all I gave her. She cut into it slowly, like it was something to be revered, before taking a bite. She ate unhurriedly, taking a small piece at a time until it was all gone. Mine, I gobbled up, dipping thick slices of fresh bread to wipe up the runny yolk.

I rinsed the dishes and set them in the dishwasher, then I brought the coffee pot to the table and refilled our mugs. Cassie looked better now, with color coming back on her cheeks. I detected a shift in her mood.

"Thanks," she said, giving me a grateful look.

"You want to talk about it?" I said.

She toyed with the mug, running her fingers across the rim.

I waited. I sensed Cassie had more feelings for this guy than she'd let on, and it wasn't because of his flair for cooking. It wasn't like Cassie to care for one guy—she'd usually have half a dozen hanging around her. Maybe it was Cassie's way of not letting any one guy get too close? What was different about this guy?

She took a sip of coffee and carefully sat the mug down. "I'm sorry you missed out this morning."

"I was looking forward to it," I said. "I feel sorry for this guy, whatever happened to him."

"Blake," she said, whispering his name.

I sensed her sadness, and something else. It wasn't shock or surprise. Maybe Cassie expected it and was resigned to what happened. I wanted to know what she knew.

She folded the napkin on the table, and then unfolded it, then repeated the motion. Something was on Cassie's mind, and she wasn't sharing.

"When was the last time you saw him?"

"Yesterday morning."

"And was it the last time you talked to him?"

She didn't answer right away. "No, he called me later. Said he'd gone out of town and was on his way back."

"What time was it?"

She picked up her cell phone to check. "It's stamped 8:58 p.m."

"So, you didn't see him?"

"No, I said I'd see him in the morning."

If he gave her his phone number, would she have his address? "Do you know where he lives?"

She nodded.

Bingo, I was right. My heart was thumping. "Can you show me?"

Cassie frowned, pulling back slightly. After a moment's hesitation, she stood up and grabbed her purse. I was right behind her.

CHAPTER ELEVEN

It turned out Blake lived in an upstairs apartment about two blocks from the food truck. When we got there, a police car was parked outside. Cassie turned off the engine and put a hand on my arm. "Let's wait," she said.

We sat in the car, across the street from the two-story clapboard building. It wasn't run down. It wasn't freshly painted, either, like some of the colorful beach houses on the street. Wooden stairs led up to a second level and a separate outside entrance.

"You've been here?" I asked.

"Yes." She didn't deny it.

"Who lives downstairs?"

"The landlord and his wife," Cassie said, then added, "And their two cats and a dog."

"You talked to them?"

"Once. The first time Blake brought me here," she said. "We met when they were outside walking their dog. We passed each other. The wife, she stopped and said hello to me."

"And?"

"Blake murmured something, and we kept going. He acted like we were in a hurry, pushing me up the stairs."

"Were you?"

"Heck, no! We went in his place and watched until they walked out of sight. He burst out, heaving in fits of laughter. I did, too. You should have seen the looks on our faces."

I allowed a chuckle to escape my lips. The two of them giggling like kids, escaping from the stern school matron or the wicked witch—in this case, the landlady.

"What's his apartment like?"

"It's fine. Came furnished, with utilities included in the rent. One of the reasons he took it. Blake didn't want to fool with furnishings or to have to turn utilities on. Besides, it was reasonable and in a good location. The closer you get to the center of town, the higher the rent."

"Good deal."

"Once Blake noticed the private entrance upstairs, he took the place so he could come and go and not run into the owners as much. He kept to himself and was quiet. Said he wasn't crazy about the landlady, but her husband was okay."

We sat and waited while the couple talked to the officer.

"Say, why don't we come back later?" Cassie asked.

"Sure … where to next?"

She started the car and sped toward the bridge. I didn't have to guess where she was headed.

CHAPTER TWELVE

The North Edge Hospital served the areas outside of the city of Caperton and the town of Lolly Beach. It was part of a dying breed of small, hundred-bed hospitals. The costs had been going up, and not enough money was coming in. Because of its prime location and prominence, it had endeared locals and tourists who didn't want to fight the traffic and drive into the city. North Edge Hospital held on, in part due to its generous donors—wealthy landowners and businesses that had a vested interest.

The sliding doors swooshed open as we approached the front entrance. Sunlight spilled in from the all-glass, floor-to-ceiling walls. The waxed floor was spotless and polished, reflecting the light. The building was well-designed—as welcoming as a hospital could be. Distinguished portraits of men lined the wall, one more prominent than the others. The receptionist was charming and polite. She asked us if we were family or friends. Cassie chatted while the receptionist looked up Blake's room number.

"Room sixteen," the woman said, pointing to the corridor, where another set of doors separated the patients from the main lobby area. "It'll be on your right."

We nodded our thanks and moved on.

When we reached the room, a guard was sitting in a chair in front of the door. I didn't know if the receptionist had failed to mention it, or if she hadn't known about the guard. Cassie turned to me and whispered, "I'll go talk to him."

I thought of the saying about catching more flies with honey, and how sweet Cassie could be. I had no doubt she could do it.

"Hello, we're here to see Blake." Cassie beamed a friendly smile as she approached the guard. "How's he doing?"

The guard had been watching us. He looked like a teenager, a kid barely out of high school. His uniform hung slackly over his belt as he sat, his slim frame slouched in the chair. His fingers curved around a clipboard. "Who wants to know?"

"Well, I'm Cassie, and this here's my friend Eve."

"Are you family?"

"We're friends ... like his family. Sometimes, it's better than family."

"I can't let you go in there."

"Can we see him for a minute?" Cassie coughed and straightened her top, which caught his attention. She took a step closer.

He shifted in his chair.

"How about a quick look?"

"Well, ma'am." He cleared his throat and started over. "I *can't* let you go in. 'Em's my orders." He stared at Cassie.

"Is there any way we could see him, *please*?"

He frowned, tilting his head. A moment later, his lips curved. "There's nothin' to say you can't stand *outside* the door and peek in." He smiled, pleased with himself for coming up with this idea.

Cassie lavished compliments while he basked in her honey-dripped words.

CHAPTER THIRTEEN

THE SIGHT OF BLAKE IN THE HOSPITAL BED MADE IT REAL for me. I had pictured him a free spirit, like Cassie. From what I could see, the guy was tall, taking the full length of the metal-framed bed. His long locks of sandy brown hair spilled on the pillow. The sheets were pulled up to his waist, over the light blue and white patterned hospital gown he was wearing. The readout on the machines blinked, monitoring his vitals. Blake's eyes were closed, and he wasn't moving. I felt like a stranger peering in where I had no right to be—meeting him this way.

Cassie flinched and sucked in her breath at the sight of Blake. She stood beside me, slightly in front. One hand gripped the frame of the open doorway. I took a few steps back to give her some space and privacy.

The guard was still watching us. I sensed his curiosity, but no ill feeling. I could see the name Kenny on the name tag pinned to his rumpled uniform.

"Will he wake up?" I asked, approaching him.

Kenny shrugged. Men didn't look at me the way they looked at Cassie, but I earned their respect with my quiet beauty and my smarts. Let's say my attractiveness grew on a person, once they got to know me better. I put my full attention on Kenny.

"You know, he makes crêpes. My friend Cassie says they're the best."

"You tried them?"

"Didn't get a chance. I just got into town yesterday."

I wanted to inquire about Blake's condition, but our conversation was interrupted.

A young man, probably in his late twenties or early thirties, with intense blue eyes and lugging a black carrying case strapped on his shoulder, strode toward us. He glanced down at a scrap of paper in his hand before moving forward, pausing beside the doorway where Cassie stood.

"Is this Blake Conway's room?"

The guard stood up, all businesslike again. "Who's asking?"

The man paused to push black glasses up his nose, where they'd slid down a sweaty slope. "Jake Thorne, *Beach Beat*."

"I'm afraid you can't go in," the guard said.

Jake eyed him, seeing the name tag. "Kenny, is it?" he asked, his voice mellow and friendly. "When can I talk to him?"

"Not today."

"Tomorrow?"

"He's in a coma, and he's not in any shape to talk.

And no visitors are allowed. Stay behind the threshold please," Kenny added, drawing a line in the air.

Jake's eyes darted in my direction. He didn't speak to me.

Cassie turned, then she released the door, letting it spring shut slowly until it closed with a soft click.

We all stood there a bit awkwardly. Finally, Cassie broke the silence.

"Thanks, Kenny," she said, flashing him a bright smile. She linked her arm in mine, and we went down the corridor the way we came.

CHAPTER FOURTEEN

We scampered outside, and as we walked toward Cassie's car, someone hollered. Cassie kept on going, but I turned around, curious to know who it was.

"Wait up, please," Jake yelled. He ran across the parking lot to catch up.

I felt sorry for the guy. If he stumbled, he'd fall flat on his face. I watched his long legs sprinting to close the gap between us. I decided to wait for him, see what was so important. Out of the corner of my eye, I glimpsed Cassie opening the car door and getting in, not waiting. Jake was huffing when he reached me. He paused to catch his breath.

"I'm sorry, I didn't catch your name," Jake said.

"Eve Sawyer," I said.

He looked at Cassie, sitting in the car. "And?"

"Are you going to quote us or something? I thought you'd have to ask for permission before you can do it."

"Sorry, no harm intended. I do it out of habit," Jake said apologetically.

I looked him over. Sensed he was sincere, not being malicious or underhanded. I'd give him a chance this time. "What's so important?" I asked casually.

"I'm working on a story about Blake's attack. Blake is a celebrity of sorts here. The word gets around in a small place like this. He's built quite a following," Jake said.

"Celebrity?"

He looked puzzled. "You've never tried his crêpes?"

"I arrived yesterday," I said. "I went there this morning to see for myself."

"Why are you in town?"

"Summer break. I'm a student at Midway College, journalism major. My friend invited me down here for a beach vacation."

Jake had a charm about him. His questions were practiced and didn't put me on edge, even though I knew he was angling for a story. He paused for a moment, lifting his eyebrow. "So, you've never met Blake before?"

"First time, and he's in a hospital gown." I guessed his next question before he spoke it. "So, you're going to ask me how come I was at the hospital?" I said, laughing.

He grinned sheepishly. "Exactly."

"My friend Cassie drove us here. Back at the food truck, we saw the yellow tape, and an onlooker said the ambulance was taking him to this hospital."

"She's a good friend of Blake's?"

"From what I can tell. Honestly, I don't know." I

mumbled something about secondhand information and reliability.

Jake reached into a wallet and pulled out a card. "I want to give you this," he said.

I took it. It was the usual business card with the newspaper's name and logo and his contact information.

"Oh, I forgot to add another number." He snatched the card back, flipped it over, and scribbled something on it. "My direct number, in case you need to reach me."

"Your cell?"

He nodded. "You can call me when Cassie is ready to talk. Tell her I'm working on a story about Blake. Maybe she has an idea who could have done something like this to him."

I changed the subject. "Jake, you know him? What's Blake like?"

He paused, wrestling with something, perhaps what to share with me and how much. "I interviewed Blake about his crêpes a while back. For a story. Of course, I had to try them. Blake said we should make it authentic. I laughed. I wasn't a fan of crêpes yet. But once I had a taste … I was hooked. It became my usual morning routine. I'd get my coffee and breakfast crêpes there."

I smiled. "You know I'm a journalism student. I'm curious about Blake. What else can you tell me?"

"We kept in touch after my article on the crêpes was published," Jake said. He paused, looking away, glancing at nothing in particular. "One day, he suggested we take a walk on the beach. Wouldn't tell me why, except to ask if I would be interested in doing a story. I was intrigued. I waited after he closed up. We got to the beach around five. By then, the crowd had thinned, and people were gathering their stuff and leaving. We walked for a while in comfortable silence."

"Did you go in the water?"

"I went to the edge of the water, catching the last bit of warmth."

"What did Blake do?"

"He was quiet at first. Then Blake started talking. He said, 'The ocean ... it comes and goes, taking back what's on the beach.' He pointed out the trash people had left in the sand. 'This trash ... when swallowed by marine life or sea birds, they can choke, suffer, or die. When tangled by six-pack rings, fishing lines or nets, they can be cut, injured, unable to eat or swim, or die. Countless tons of this trash end up polluting the ocean for many years to come. In the chain from production to waste, plastics affect us, our health, our climate and our planet.'"

"What kind of trash did people leave?"

"Oh, you name it—cigarette butts, food containers, pieces of foil. All sorts of discarded plastics—water and soda bottles and caps, uncut six-pack rings, grocery bags, snack and candy wrappers, broken fishing lines and lures. I could go on and on."

"So Blake Conway, he's much more than a crêpe chef?" Cassie hadn't mentioned this part about him. I wondered if she knew how passionate he was about the environment. "What happened next?"

"Blake wrote an eloquent letter to the editor on the dangers of plastics and how they harm living creatures and our planet. He outlined his proposal to ban plastics on the beach. After the ordinance was drafted, he got a sponsor, drummed up support, and met with town council members. He challenged the citizens to do their part and vote to keep the beaches beautiful—clean, safe, and litter-free—and to fine violators who discard plastics."

"Did he have support?"

"Yes, he talked to his customers and anyone who'd listen. After Blake closed in the afternoons, he went door-to-door talking to people and handing out flyers and information."

"Did he have help?"

"Larry in the burger food truck and some of his customers. One of his most devoted supporters was a regular."

"Who was he?"

"You've seen the guy wearing the orange T-shirt?"

I nodded. "The guy who was first in line at the food truck and went inside to check on Blake this morning?"

"That's him."

"Was there a public meeting?" I asked.

"At the town hall. Ended up getting quite a large turnout."

I smiled. "It's so cool you guys got the ban on plastics passed."

He gave me an odd look. "The vote hasn't been taken yet. It's scheduled next week."

I asked Jake the question I'd been dying to ask.

"What do you think happened today? Did Blake have enemies?"

"I got to know the man behind the quiet exterior. This guy is sharp, decisive, and conscientious. He's strong willed and intrepid. He sets his goals and goes after them, sometimes to the point of being obstinate." Jake fiddled with a pen, his thumb pressing the button in rapid succession. The clicking sound filled the air. He appeared to be getting more and more agitated. "Oh God, Blake," he cried out hoarsely.

I sensed Jake's pain and more. From the way he talked, they had spent time together and developed a camaraderie, a closeness to the point he and Blake could trust one another on a personal level.

He coughed, clearing his throat. "This whole thing with the proposed local ordinance … it wasn't all smooth sailing. Some irate people spoke at the public hearing. They were few but quite vocal."

"Someone at the meeting did this to him?"

"I don't know, but I'm going to look at the meeting transcripts this afternoon. I'll interview the people who spoke out against the proposed ordinance."

"Mind if I tag along?" The words flew out of my mouth before I'd finished thinking. "I mean, I'd be an observer."

Jake paused and stared at me.

"Give me another card," I said. I crossed out his information and wrote my name and cell below it. "Here's mine."

Jake studied it before he carefully tucked it away.

"It wasn't so long ago when I was your age in

college, dreaming of majoring in journalism and changing the world," he said, smiling. "I reckon it's your turn. Be ready early tomorrow morning. We'll get started on the interviews."

My heart was thumping against my chest. I folded my arms to calm it. I gulped. "Where shall we meet?"

"Come to my house," he said. "I'll text you the address."

Jake took a deep breath and opened his mouth again. I guessed he wasn't done talking yet. "A couple of days ago, Blake dropped a hint. I believe he was testing the water."

"For this plastics ban?"

"He asked if I was interested in doing an investigative story and had I ever done one."

"Have you?"

Jake nodded. "I told him I was part of an investigative journalism team in a big city newspaper, in my previous life."

"What did he say?"

"He wanted to know why I left."

I was curious how Jake ended up working on a beach newspaper, but I didn't want to pry.

"I told Blake I was a reporter for a big paper. When an opportunity came up to work on investigative stories, I joined the team. We worked hard, long days and nights, chasing down leads and doing interviews. I got robbed one night. I fought back and was injured and ended up in a hospital for surgery. Afterward, I decided to make a change. Get out of the city. Go to a small town. Breathe fresh air. When I left, I kept my contacts in the city," Jake said.

"Will you go back?"

He shrugged. "I'm staying here, for now."

I could understand. A traumatic event affected not only the body, but also the mind. They both needed time to heal, and it might take years. "Did Blake give you a hint?" I gently prodded.

"He gave me a hypothetical. 'What if ... what if someone had information about corporate secrets or cover ups? Where would they take it?' I said it depends. What information did they have?"

"What did he say?"

"He said he'd get back to me."

"Did he?" I asked.

"No, it was the last time I talked to him," Jake murmured softly.

"Do you still want to talk to Cassie?" I asked. Jake had two choices. Either he could question Cassie today, or he could let her be for now. I waited. Cassie had choices, too. She could decide not to talk to him at all.

"Well, that's a question for another day," he said, straightening the strap on his shoulder.

"I don't know how much she can tell you. I mean, what happened to Blake was a surprise to Cassie as much as the rest of us," I said, my thoughts turning to the man in the hospital.

"If Cassie feels like talking in a day or two, please call me."

"Sure," I said.

He took a step back, turning to pull out a newspaper from the shoulder bag. It was slightly crumpled, the corners curled and turned up. "Our weekly paper, *Beach Beat*." He pointed to a story on the front page.

Jake's name was under the story headline, "Popular New Crêpe Chef on Lolly Beach." There was a picture of Blake standing with a wide grin in front of the food truck. I leaned in to get a closer look at his face, the first time I'd seen it. He looked happy, his smile unsuspecting.

CHAPTER FIFTEEN

MY STOMACH MADE AN ANNOUNCEMENT WHEN I OPENED the car door and slid in the passenger seat. I realized I was famished. "How about a late lunch? You know I could eat again and not have to worry about my weight," I said.

"I know just the place," Cassie said, cheering up a bit from either my presence or the thought of having warm, comforting food in her tummy.

"Let's go," I said.

We ended up on the pier, having lunch in a cute, touristy restaurant overlooking the ocean. We were seated at a table right above the water as the waves splashed and swirled, tumbling around the thick, long poles of the pier. Overhead was a clear blue sky with not a cloud in sight. A gentle breeze ruffled my hair and brought a refreshing coolness and reprieve from the humidity. I smelled the ocean and could almost taste the brine.

Despite the warmth of the day and the bright sun, I

felt a sense of gloom sitting under the shade of the awning. Maybe it was the way Cassie sat, head slightly bowed. Maybe it was the sight of Blake, alone in the hospital room. Could he have heard us even though he was in a coma? Maybe someone had tried to kill him and thought he was dead. Would the person come back to finish the job once they realized Blake wasn't dead?

I'd worked hard all semester. All I wanted now was some R & R at the beach. To soak up the sun, feel the ocean breeze, and listen to the waves crashing. To do nothing but eat, sleep, and relax.

My inner sense, though, had a mind of its own. It wouldn't listen to me or to reason. When something or someone disturbed the peace, it drove me to get to the truth of the matter, even if there was danger. Especially where there was a sadness or great injustice. I guess it was like a sixth sense, but I didn't believe it was developed yet, and I didn't really know how to use it. It preoccupied my thoughts until I had to act. It overrode what I did, even if it led to a darkness where I didn't want to go. I couldn't shake off the sense of foreboding, which could get in the way and take me down a murky path. Yet, there might be no other path to take.

I sighed and reached out to touch Cassie's hand. It was on the table, limp, half-curled on its side, fingers clutching the edge of the napkin.

She looked up, acknowledging me. Her eyes were moistened.

"Do you want to talk about it?" I asked.

Cassie stared at the crumpled napkin as if the answers were written on it, shaking her head.

"It'll be all right," I said, patting her hand like a mother soothing her child's hurt. I didn't know what else to say. I'd never seen Cassie this way. I felt there was a big gap I wasn't privy to. It didn't make sense otherwise. Why would anyone react this way to a casual acquaintance, even if it was their favorite food truck chef? Was his cooking so good, she was mourning over it? It had to be something else. The way she looked at Blake back in the hospital room, her face blanched, lips pinched. Her fingers had gripped the door frame so tight, it looked like her knuckles would pop out.

CHAPTER SIXTEEN

I HELPED AN EXHAUSTED CASSIE INTO BED FOR A NAP, and I made sure she was sound asleep before I left. I walked back toward the center of town, retracing our route from this morning. The sun was blazing hot, the temperature at its highest. I took small steps, plodding steadily along, not rushing to get anywhere fast.

My footsteps led me to the parking lot where Blake's food truck was parked. Someone had closed the door and plastered it with more yellow tape. There were a half-dozen other food trucks in this lot. The closest one advertised smoothie drinks, and the one on the other side of Blake's had hot dogs, burgers, and fries. The line in front of the smoothie truck was long, so I ambled toward the other one, which had one person in line.

"What'll you have?" the kid asked when it was my turn, his apron smudged with grease marks. The smell of fried food wafted over, tempting me. I didn't eat meat, but it had never stopped me from finding something on the menu I could have.

"How about a big order of fries," I said.

"Tell you what, I'm going to make you a fresh batch," he said, tossing out the soggy-looking fries in the fryer basket.

I grinned. "Make my day."

He opened a bag of frozen fries and dumped the contents into the basket, whistling while he worked.

"Be ready in a few minutes," he said, coming back to the window.

"I'm in no hurry," I said. "Like your job?"

"Yeah, it's a good gig."

"Hang out at the beach much?"

"I'm done with this at three," he said. "And you're my last customer."

"Well, lucky me. I'm Eve. What's your name?"

"Larry."

"I was here this morning," I said, pointing at the crêpe truck. "Sorry about what happened to Blake."

"Gosh, it sure was awful." He took off his cap and ran his fingers through his thick brown hair before slipping the cap back on.

"What do you make of it?"

"I dunno. Blake's a nice guy as far as I can tell."

"Who'd want to do this?"

"Could be anybody, I guess," he said, then nervously chuckled. "I hope it's not an angry customer."

"Has it happened here before?"

"Well, no. Not that I know of."

"Has anyone gotten mad, upset, angry at Blake?"

He thought for a moment. "No."

"Anything weird?"

"Well, there was this one guy ..." The ding of the timer sounded, and he looked relieved to be saved by the bell.

"A beach guy?" I asked, squeezing in a quick question while trying not to sound urgent.

"A man in a suit, looked out of place here."

Larry disappeared, then returned with a generous portion of fries. He pointed to the ketchup bottle and napkins in a basket on the ledge.

"Help yourself," Larry said.

"Thank you," I said, and squeezed the bottle, dumping a thick wad of ketchup on my fries. A small table with a couple of dusty plastic chairs stood in the corner of the lot, and I made my way there.

There was nothing like hot, greasy french fries. I ate quickly, like a greedy kid, until I was done taking the last bite. Those fries were mighty tasty, and I could eat anything I wanted and not have to worry about my weight.

I sat back, satiated, and scanned the surroundings.

CHAPTER SEVENTEEN

IT WAS THE NEON ORANGE THAT CAUGHT MY ATTENTION. I recognized the T-shirt as the guy crossed the parking lot to the street, walking away and holding a cup in one hand. I flew out of my seat.

"Wait!"

He didn't stop or turn around.

I sped up, focusing on the bright color like a bull's-eye. He slowed to take a sip of his drink. I caught up with him.

The guy was older than I thought at first glance. His sunburnt face held a few lines, now squinting an exasperated, *do I know you* look, not quite irritated or amused, or welcoming.

"I'm sorry. I recognized you from this morning," I said, smiling cheerfully. I didn't hold out my hand since he was occupied with his drink. "I'm Eve. I was at the crêpe truck this morning. You were there."

"Didn't see ya," he muttered.

"I was in the back." I paused. "My friend is bummed

out. I was hoping I could talk to you—you know, if you can help us out."

"What'ya want from me?"

I took a breath and steadied my breathing. "We're worried about Blake. I understand you were the one who found him this morning."

He nodded.

"You're his friend?" I asked.

His cool demeanor defrosted a bit, like his drink. I watched the condensation roll down the cup, dripping water on his fingers. He sized me up before he spoke. "Yeah, you could say that. I'm his customer, a regular." He coughed up a soft laugh. "We even hung out together."

"Did you know he was making a special crêpe today?"

"How could I not know? Blake was so excited. Made me promise not to tell the lucky lady."

I wasn't sure I heard right. "Special crêpe for a lady?"

He broke into a smile. I could see his teeth were uneven. I'd bet they'd never met an orthodontist. I sensed he was slow to warm up, but once he'd decided he could trust you, he'd be a loyal friend. "I got here real early, ya know, to see it first."

"You found Blake?"

He nodded solemnly, not speaking.

"Where was he?"

"He was on the floor inside the truck. I didn't know if he was dead or alive." He paused, his shoe kicking free a half-buried pebble in the road.

"Go on," I said softly.

He bent his head. "I ain't a praying man. Went to church as a kid, but I've been long gone since. I haven't asked God for nothin'," he said. Raising his head, his hazel eyes stared into mine. "When I was alone inside his food truck, alone with my friend, I thought he was dead."

I was drawn to this stranger, felt a connection.

"You know what? I ain't never been with a dead person. I couldn't touch him." His voice quivered.

"How did you know if he was alive or not? Did you check his pulse?"

"I ain't touched him," he said, with a belligerent firmness. "I was shakin' up and scared."

"What did you do?"

"I moved slow like this and held a finger under his nose," he said, motioning.

"And?"

"He was still breathin'. I was so relieved, I was. I kept repeatin', 'Thank God.' I stayed there, rockin' on my knees."

I let it soak in. Gave him room. A moment of comfortable silence wrapped around us.

"I'm sorry, I never asked your name," I said.

"Jeremiah," he said, and smiled shyly. "My friends call me Jeb."

"Well, Jeb," I said, holding my hand out. "Nice to make your acquaintance."

He blushed. I shook his hand a moment longer, feeling the callused and hardened skin of a working man.

I tore off a piece of napkin and scribbled my name and cell phone number on it. "Jeb, you can call me anytime. If you think of something or want to talk, call me, okay?"

He took the torn napkin and looked at my number. "Ya gonna help him?"

Part of me wanted to return to the beach, relax and have fun. I knew I couldn't and wouldn't have any peace—not when Blake was fighting for his life in the hospital, and Cassie was despondent and hurting. My sixth sense prodded me.

"I'm gonna help him," I finally said. "Can I have your number?"

Walking away with Jeb's information added to my phone's contacts, I thought of a question and turned around. "Hey, Jeb, you know who the lucky lady is?"

"Huh?"

"The girl, you know her name?"

Jeb hesitated.

"Did Blake tell you?"

"Yeah," Jeb said, looking down. "But I can't say."

CHAPTER EIGHTEEN

A BEAT-UP LOOKING TRUCK WAS PARKED IN FRONT OF the beach house. Bare rust spots, scratches, and small dents marred its blue paint. I quickened my pace, eager to meet our visitor.

The front door was open. Laughter drifted from inside. Cassie sounded cheerful, almost like her old self. Then I heard a male voice, rich and deep.

"I'm here," I announced as I barged in. I recognized the voice a split second before the familiar head of unruly hair popped into view.

Bob turned around. He grinned when he saw me. "Hi, Eve." His welcoming hazel eyes radiated warmth.

Sometimes, Bob was so quiet, we'd almost forgotten he was with us in the lab. Cassie and I had chatted away excitedly about our beach getaway as we neared the end of the semester. Bob had overheard. Well, he couldn't *help* overhearing. At some point, he jokingly asked if we had room for one more. I thought we had bored the heck out of Bob. It was no joke. He wanted to come. I'd caught Cassie's eye and nodded enthusiastically. It was all it took. She invited him.

"So glad you made it," I said, giving him a quick hug.

"And you, you gave up your room for me," Bob said.

I laughed. "You wish …"

"Let's take your stuff in there and get you settled," Cassie said.

Bob had traveled light. He picked up the duffel bag at his feet.

We paused at the doorway of my room. I was relieved I made my bed every morning, thankful for my upbringing. Cassie had taken hold of Bob's arm and was pulling him away. I grabbed his other arm and pulled him in the room, as he stood with legs straddled on each side of the doorway. We tugged, and he leaned one way and the other as we laughed playfully. He took it pretty well when we finally showed him to his bedroom—the closet. It was like old times, the three of us working together in the lab. Bob's arrival was a welcome respite.

❧

WHILE DINNER WAS COOKING on the stove, Cassie updated Bob about Blake and everything that had happened. I chimed in a few times as I heated up the frying pan and slid in pats of butter to sauté the fresh shrimp for our main entrée. I cut up tomatoes and carrots and tossed in mixed greens for a salad. In no time at all, we were sitting down to eat.

I filled Cassie in about my conversation with Jake

and gave her a heads up that he'd like to interview her in the next couple of days. She didn't object. We discussed what we were going to do the next day. Cassie would give Bob a tour of the town in the morning, and they'd spend the afternoon on the beach. I could tell Bob was thrilled and ready. He was a meticulous type of guy who came prepared with suntan lotion and beach flip-flops. I mentioned I'd be out of the house early to tag along on Jake's interviews. I didn't tell them we might be facing some angry people.

CHAPTER NINETEEN

I TOSSED AND TURNED BEFORE I FELL ASLEEP. PART OF me was excited, and part of me was anxious. My mind was working overtime. Would Jake and I come face-to-face tomorrow with the person who attacked Blake? Did someone want to silence him because of his actions on the ordinance to ban plastics? The timing was suspect. Or was it a mere coincidence?

When the alarm sounded on my phone, I jumped out of bed, got dressed, and brushed my teeth. I brewed coffee and made a quick breakfast of scrambled eggs and toast. I grabbed my notebook and a couple of water bottles as I ran out the door to meet Jake. Last night, he had texted the address of his house and was expecting me there at nine o'clock.

❧

JAKE WAS outside on his porch when I pulled in his driveway, a bag slung over his shoulder. His place was a small cottage, neatly painted light blue. A postage-sized trimmed yard surrounded the house in the narrow lot. It looked down-to-earth and quietly unassuming, without the colorful gaudiness of some decked beach houses I'd seen.

I waved, rolled down the window, and shouted, "I can drive. Shall we take my car?"

He nodded and strode to the car, crossing over to the passenger side.

I leaned over the seat and pulled the handle, popping the door open.

"Good morning, Eve," Jake said as he settled in, putting his bag on the floor between his legs.

I caught the faint scent of his aftershave and noticed he had shaved. His hair was fluffy and damp from the shower. His shirt looked like it was freshly laundered and pressed.

Jake unzipped his shoulder bag and took out a notebook, flipping to find the page. He tapped it with a pen. "I have the addresses of three people who voiced the loudest objections at the public hearing. Two of them are men, and one is a woman. Are you ready?"

"Yes, can't wait."

"Let's go with the first name, Leonard Clay," Jake said. He gave me directions while I drove.

WE KNOCKED on the door of a clapboard house slightly in need of paint. A wooden, gaudy-looking painted fish was nailed to the post above a mailbox. Other than that, the house was devoid of outside decoration.

Leonard turned out to be an older man, with a head of mostly white hair and an untrimmed beard. He came to the door dressed in a wrinkled shirt and overalls with roomy, deep pockets.

Jake pulled out his ID. "Jake Thorne, *Beach Beat*."

The man studied the ID and grunted. He looked at me. "Who's this?"

"Eve Sawyer, journalism student," Jake said, introducing me. "Leonard, I understand you were at the public meeting on the proposed beach ordinance to ban plastics. I'd like to ask you a few questions."

"I done said what I said at the meetin'."

"Mr. Clay, you're a fisherman?" Jake asked.

Leonard drew up his chest and pulled his overall clasp tighter. "You damn right—been fifty years since my Daddy showed me how to fish when I's a boy."

"Did you grow up around here?"

"Born an' raised."

"You fish on the pier or the beach?"

"Both," Leonard said.

"Did you oppose the plastics ban ordinance because you fish on the beach?"

"Nobody can tell me not to fish there."

"There's no ban on fishing. It's the disposal of fishing lines—leaving the plastics on the beach."

"I can fish where I want to and cut my lines and do what I do. Ain't *nobody* gonna stop me. Now leave me be," Leonard said, raising his voice. He took a menacing step toward us. “Get off my property!” His angry glare fixated on us as we retreated.

CHAPTER TWENTY

THE SECOND PERSON ON THE LIST, SANDY DAYNE, wasn't home when we knocked on his door, so we moved on to the last one, a woman named Bea Johnson. I pictured her to be a matronly, middle-aged woman, but I couldn't have been more wrong. Knocking on the door, we heard yelling and a baby crying inside. The woman who opened the door was young and thin, carrying a baby in one arm, hoisted over a hip. My guess was Bea was in her early to mid-twenties. Jake and I introduced ourselves, then he did his spiel.

"Ma'am," he said politely. "Ms. Johnson, at the public meeting, you spoke against the proposed beach ordinance. Do you know Blake Conway?"

She looked away, distracted by the crying, snot-nosed toddler pulling on her dress.

I wondered if she thought about the future of her kids when she spoke. Did she care about the earth and the environmental legacy left for them?

"Oh, shut up," Bea said to the wailing toddler cleaved to her, clamoring for her attention.

She turned to Jake. "I ain't got no time to talk."

"We want to ask why you spoke out," Jake said.

Bea reshuffled the baby in her arms. "Can't you see? The government's going to use it to tax us."

"What do you mean?"

"Who's going to pay for the extra clean-up? How many people they gonna hire?" Bea questioned. She raised her voice. "Did ya think of that . . . *huh*?"

The door slammed in our faces. I jumped at the loud bang. We weren't any closer to finding out what happened to Blake.

"You figure one of these people did it?" I asked.

"They're both angry for different reasons," Jake said.

I doubted either of these people was going to listen to reason by way of scientific evidence. They had their minds made up. Was it enough to want to hurt Blake? Was it meant as a warning to stop him? Or did the perpetrator mean to kill him? I thought of Blake lying in the hospital bed in a coma.

"Let's go back and check on the second person; maybe he's home now," Jake said, getting in the car. "We can look around. Talk to the neighbors and find out when was the last time they saw him."

Sounded like a plan to me.

CHAPTER TWENTY-ONE

We went back to Sandy Dayne's house. It looked the same as before. The carport was empty. I turned to look at Jake, my hand clasped on the seat belt release. He was still strapped in.

"Hey, kid. Why do you want to study journalism?" Jake asked.

I bristled at the mention of the word "kid." I was twenty years old, for Pete's sake. A young but grown-up woman. I could easily replace kid with mature, intelligent, strong—a sometimes pencil-chewing neurotic with a heart of gold and curiosity to poke my nose in things and, um, stir them up. I could throw in knock-out gorgeous, but it'd be stretching the truth. My face was somewhere between unique-looking and alluring, with a trace of Asian in my European blood. I tumbled out of my mother's womb with a head chock-full of light brown hair. It'd turned shades darker since, but it was the first thing anyone noticed about me, to this day.

"I'm curious by nature and inspired by justice, peace, truth, and making this world a better place," I said.

"Tall order, kid, and idealistic," he said.

"Please don't call me a kid."

Jake stared at me. I hoped he was taking a good look and realizing I was a grown woman, and quite a capable one.

"All right, Eve," he said. He held out his hand to shake mine, like man to man. "No hard feelings?"

"No, sir," I said, smiling.

He unclasped his seat belt and opened the car door. "Let's go."

We circled around the property to the back. The windows and the back door were closed. The lights were out. We didn't see anyone and went around to the front again.

"Hey, can I help you?" a man shouted from the driveway next door.

Jake was ready, his ID badge already pulled out. "Jake Thorne, *Beach Beat*. We're looking for Sandy Dayne."

"He ain't here."

"Have you seen him today?"

The man rubbed his jaw, running his hand over stubble. "I ain't seen him lately. He comes and goes."

"Can you tell us where to find him?"

"I don't ask him no questions."

"Know where he works?"

The man shook his head. "He's done odd jobs here and there. He ain't said nothin' to me."

"Can you give him a message when he comes back?" Jake pulled out a business card and handed it to the man. "Have him call me, please."

The man nodded.

"What's your name?"

"Ralph," the man said. "They call me Big Ralph."

CHAPTER TWENTY-TWO

We spent the next few hours at the library. Jake had his laptop with him. I'd left mine at the beach house, and I didn't want to go back for it. I used the computer in the library.

I checked the three people on our list. I first came across an old article about Leonard Clay. Some years back, he had caught a fish that broke the town's record. There was a picture of a much younger Leonard proudly holding it. On close scrutiny, and if I squinted extra hard, I visualized a faint resemblance between the photo and the wooden fish nailed to his house post.

A few incidents popped up when I did a search on Bea. She had been in some trouble with the law, minor shoplifting and truancy when she was a teenager. Nothing since then. I didn't find anything on Sandy.

Time had crept up on me. Jake had left me undisturbed. I went back to the table where he worked on his laptop. I flopped down on the chair beside him.

"Find anything?" Jake asked.

"Not much. An old article of Leonard making the news on breaking the town's record, and Bea had some misdemeanors."

"A record?"

"For the biggest fish caught," I said. "What about you?"

Jake pushed his laptop toward me. "Take a look at this."

There was a big headline. "Young Entrepreneur of the Year." I quickly skimmed the article. Apparently, Blake had been doing well. The photo showed a handsome young man, hair perfectly cut, dressed in an expensive tailored suit, accepting the award at a fancy gala. The words "youngest and brightest" caught my attention.

Blake was quoted as saying he was an ideas guy and chose his projects carefully. First and foremost, he had to be passionate before he invested time, effort, and money in anything. It wasn't about the money. He wanted to leave a lasting legacy. One that gave back to the people and reinvested in the earth and the future. Blake liked to get first-hand impressions on projects, and he didn't rely totally on numbers or surveys. He didn't spend all his time behind a desk. Blake was young, energetic, creative, and fearless. The article didn't mention he wanted to be a chef.

I scrolled down to the end of the article to be sure I hadn't missed anything. Was this the same guy? The Blake we knew was a crêpe chef in a food truck. How did a guy like this end up here?

CHAPTER TWENTY-THREE

JAKE CLOSED HIS LAPTOP AND PUT IT BACK IN THE shoulder bag. "It's about twelve-thirty. Wanna grab something to eat?" He'd changed the subject. What else did he come across in his research?

On the other hand, lunch sounded great. I was not one to refuse food. I may have been on the thin side, but it wasn't because I counted calories. Quite the opposite.

Jake picked a sandwich shop. It was a hole-in-the-wall place tucked behind a row of stores in a prime real estate location. By the time we got there, the lunch crowd had thinned, and we found a small table quickly. He had a turkey and cheese sandwich, and I munched on a tuna fish salad. The food was good.

I pushed my empty plate away and sat back in the chair.

"Do you miss the big-city daily newspaper?"

"In some ways, I miss the excitement of a city newsroom and thrill of landing the big scoop. But the daily grind and stress isn't for the weak. Besides, working at a small-town paper has its charm." Jake smiled. "I get to enjoy the beach, and I only have one deadline a week."

I made a mental note, putting this information away for when the time came after I graduated. He didn't mention the challenges in a small weekly. I imagined they'd be different here. Maybe I'd find out later.

I updated Jake on what I'd found out the day before, talking to the other food truck vendors. I mentioned the man in the suit, and the conversations I had with Larry and Jeremiah. I added their names to the list of three people.

"What else did you dig up in your research?" I asked.

"More articles about Blake after winning his award. The story was picked up by other papers, and there were follow-ups. I have a timeline to work from now, except for a short gap between leaving his office and opening his crêpe food truck here," Jake said.

"Anything on his early life?"

"Not much. He was adopted as a baby. Never knew his real parents. I think he was an average student. Blake told me he didn't apply himself to his studies. He was restless and bored easily. I know he's intelligent."

"Private or public school?"

"He went to mostly private schools. Expensive, I think."

"Was he an only child?"

"Blake had mentioned his parents had a baby girl when he was two."

"Did they get along?"

"Blake talked about her and said she adored her big brother. She was close to him, and they had happy childhoods. They got along fine. The children were both loved, but things changed for Blake after the little girl was born and his parents turned their attention to the baby. The adoption was kept from both children until they were grown. It was a shock when they found out. After college, the two drifted apart." Jake paused, shaking his head. "I don't know exactly what happened. Blake didn't tell me. Maybe they had an argument. My guess is it was shortly after they learned about Blake's adoption. I think it was a disappointment to him. He pulled away after he found out."

"Are his parents still alive?"

"His father is, but Blake said his mother had passed away a couple of years ago," Jake said. "His father was a successful business man, and his mother never worked outside the home."

"Where's his sister?"

"She graduated from college and went to work for a big company."

"Which one?"

"Thirst, a soft drink company. Ever heard of their new line of thirst quenchers?"

"Who hasn't? They're everywhere."

"It's her baby. Got her a raise and noticed. Rumor is she's being considered for one of the VP positions."

"Family? Kids?"

"She never married. Threw herself into work."

"His father ... do they talk to each other?'

"Blake said they had a falling out. Family split after the parents told the kids. It was never the same since then."

"How sad," I said, remembering Blake in the hospital bed. Would he want to see and talk to them, if and when he ever came out of his coma?

CHAPTER TWENTY-FOUR

I INVITED JAKE TO THE BEACH HOUSE AFTER LUNCH. I had called Cassie and given her a heads up when we'd be there. I thought she and Bob might want to meet Jake and vice-versa.

I pulled up to the driveway behind Cassie's car. We got out, and I led the way to the door. Bob was waiting for us and held the screen door open. Cassie was in the kitchen putting away some things. After introductions, we sat around the kitchen table and got caught up. Bob didn't say much and just listened, soaking it all in. He liked to mull over things and chew on them before jumping in with assumptions. I knew Cassie would be interested in Jake's research, and it'd be an opportunity to ask Cassie questions, too.

I watched Cassie as Jake talked about Blake's family. She nodded a few times, as if she was familiar with parts of the story. I didn't know how much Blake had shared his family's story with Cassie. When Jake was done, she let out a huge sigh.

“Did you know about his family?” Jake asked.

“Blake told me pretty much the same thing,” Cassie said. “I knew about his family.”

“Ever meet them?”

“No.”

“Mind if I ask you some questions?” Jake said.

“Shoot.”

“Did Blake tell you why he left to come here?”

“Not in so many words,” Cassie said.

“Were you surprised he received this prestigious award?”

“It’s well deserved. He’s certainly earned it.”

“Any idea why Blake came to this place? Was he looking for new business opportunities? Taking some time off? Or running away from something or somebody?”

“I don’t know.”

“He never mentioned it?”

“Not that. You know he’s creative, always drumming up new ideas and ways to do things. Maybe he wanted to recharge his batteries or change direction.”

“It appears he had other talents … as a chef,” Jake said.

Cassie brightened. “The first time I met him, he dared me to try his crêpes,” she said, laughing. “He has a sense of humor. Made me laugh. I thought he was another beach bum at first. It wasn’t until later, after I got to know him better, that I found out he owned the food truck and was a successful businessman.”

“He didn’t mention if he was worried about anything?” Jake asked.

"He didn't say, at least not in so many words."

"What do you mean?"

"There were moments when I thought he wanted to tell me something ..." Cassie said.

"But he didn't?"

"No."

CHAPTER TWENTY-FIVE

I DECIDED TO GO TO THE BEACH WITH CASSIE AND BOB. With all the stuff going on, I hadn't had a chance to hang out with them. And a relaxing soak in the sun would help. We invited Jake, but he declined. Said he had other things to do. Perhaps he didn't go to the beach much, even if he lived here and could go anytime.

We all piled in Bob's pickup, and he drove with our beach chairs and umbrellas in the back. Bob was curious about Blake and wanted to visit him in the hospital. We made plans to spend time at the beach, then head back to the house later in the afternoon to shower off and change into more appropriate attire before visiting Blake.

❧

I DOZED off for a while on the beach chair. The sun had shifted, and the shade retreated as the rays bore down on me. I woke up in a sweat. Squinting to look for Cassie and Bob, I caught sight of their heads in the water, bobbing up and down with the waves. At this time of the day, the beach was crowded. Colorful umbrellas decked the sand. Kids were playing, yelling in excitement, running with little plastic shovels and buckets and building sand castles. I noticed the litter—discarded cartons, plastic drink bottles, food wrappers, snack bags, toys, and other items strewn everywhere.

My eyes caught a familiar label, the one I'd seen on billboards, magazine ads, and on TV, the one with Thirst in large print. I scrutinized it with new interest. I remembered the ads. A shower of water drops and an elated girl, lips parted, about to quench her thirst. They were eye-catching, striking ads, which had stuck out in the crowded market of soft drinks. They threw money into the marketing, and it had worked. The new line of drinks was in the playing field with the big guys, taking a chunk of their market shares.

It wasn't the lure of a wholesome, pretty girl on the label, it was more. Thirst actually tasted great, plus electrolytes and minerals had been added to the drink, along with other desirable ingredients. Things other soft drinks didn't have. And it wasn't cheap. I remembered when a new brand of coffee came out, and coffee shops were selling them at four bucks a cup. People snickered. But pretty soon, plenty of people reached in their pockets for four dollars. Every day.

Thirst was *that* good.

CHAPTER TWENTY-SIX

WE HAD DINNER FIRST BEFORE GOING TO THE HOSPITAL. On the way there, Cassie picked up a bouquet of fresh flowers. We didn't talk much on the way over. It was a somber, solemn moment. I had pushed the image of Blake lying on the hospital bed from my mind. I didn't want to believe he could get worse. A selfish part of me wanted him to be alive and to make crêpes for me. But I wasn't the doctor. How long would he stay in a coma? Was he in pain? Would he wake up with his memory intact? My mind was filled with unanswered questions. I glanced at Cassie. She was quiet, lost in thought, frowning. I reached out to clasp her hand.

Bob was good at directions, and he liked to drive. We arrived at the hospital in good time and got out. We headed straight down the corridor. I wondered if the same guard would be there.

I was first in line as the door in the corridor swung open automatically. I looked to the right, toward

Blake's room. Kenny was in his usual spot. He stood when we approached and nodded in recognition.

"Hi, Kenny," I said.

His shoulders straightened at the sound of his name. A smile played on his lips.

"How is he?" I asked.

"He's about the same," Kenny said. "But you still can't go in."

Cassie pushed open the door to Blake's room, and we peeked in. She held out the flowers to Kenny. "Could you do me a favor and put them in his room … please?"

He hesitated. Maybe this was a new situation he hadn't encountered before. I doubted it was in his instructions or protocol book, if there was one. Maybe Kenny wasn't sure if *he* could go in?

Or maybe it was because Blake's eyes were shut, and he wouldn't be able to see the flowers.

"It's something to keep him company, since he can't have visitors," Cassie said softly.

Kenny took the flowers and slipped into the room, placing the vase on the table next to Blake. I watched to see if Blake moved, but he didn't. He was tethered to the machines, still in a coma.

Cassie murmured a "thank you" as Kenny passed us on his way back. I sensed her sadness, her energy levels plummeting along with any hopes she had of Blake getting better. There was nothing she or any of us could do.

Kenny went back to his station. I wondered what he

thought—and if he really knew anything about Blake's condition, would he tell us?

I stepped back, bumping into Bob looking over our heads.

Sniffles came from Cassie. A whimper escaped. She twisted her lips, trying to be brave, holding back the sobs. She didn't attempt to leave, not yet. I stood next to Cassie for support and sensed her pain for this man who was more of a mystery to me now than ever.

Maybe it was the sound of Cassie's crying or the intensity of our gaze. Maybe the flowers had something to do with it. The beep of the machine startled us, alerting the nurses at the station. The corridor door swooshed open, and two nurses rushed toward us. At the same time, Kenny was snapping at us to step aside.

I pushed Cassie out of the way as Bob and I scurried to clear the entrance. The situation became more urgent. More machines were beeping, and red lights blinking. Another person in scrubs joined the nurses as they gathered around the hospital bed, working frantically on Blake, blocking our view.

"You need to leave now," Kenny said. His firm voice was authoritative and non-negotiable.

CHAPTER TWENTY-SEVEN

Bob dropped me off at the food truck lot and took Cassie home. I called Jake. I heard the surprise in his voice when he picked up, but it quickly turned to concern when I explained what happened. Was this a turn for the worse or something else? Would Blake survive?

Jake said he'd called a contact at the police station, a man named Perry. Most of the crimes in this small beach town were minor, like shoplifting and occasional vandalism, and often attributed to the teenage kids and pranksters. Serious and violent crimes were few and far between. Perry was someone he'd met covering the stories, and they had developed a professional relationship. I supposed it'd be handy sometimes.

❧

I ordered a fruit smoothie and took it to the table and sat down. Same spot where I was the day before. I needed a place to pull my thoughts together, and this spot was as good as any. In the back of my mind, I hoped to catch the perp. They always went back to the scene of the crime, didn't they? I placed another call. This time to Jeb.

"Blake's gotten worse," I blurted out.

"Is this Eve?"

I nodded, glad he couldn't see my face. "Uh-huh."

"You're okay?"

"I guess. Thought you'd like to know."

There was a pause on the other end. "Ya went to see him?"

"Yes, twice."

"Look, I'm glad ya called," Jeb said. "Ya know … the other day after we talked, I thought of somethin'."

"Yeah?"

"Well, I tripped over a peach … almost fell stepping over the doorway of the truck. I's angry, kicked it under the counter. I woke up last night, couldn't sleep. I thought it was odd, this peach in my dream."

"Okay," I said.

"I's couldn't figure out what it was doing there. Then it came to me."

"What?"

"The peach had to be the surprise. Blake said he was going to make a special crêpe."

"Did you see only one peach?"

"'Em's more. I saw 'em in a paper bag."

"A bag from the market here?"

"Naw, it had 'em rope handles."

"Did you see a label or logo?"

"It had a sticker ... a cartoon drawing of a rising sun and a basket of fruit."

"Any writing?"

"Don't know. I glanced at it for a sec, trying to avoid stepping on anythin'."

Another call was coming in. I ended the call with Jeb to grab it. It was Jake. Why was he calling me back?

"Hey," I said in my chirpy voice. I was in a good mood with this new piece of information. I couldn't wait to tell Jake.

"Where are you?"

"At the food truck lot getting a smoothie."

"Well, you'd better get home now."

"What?" I stopped in mid-air, the straw inches from my lips. A sense of dread swooped down. My heart tightened. A chill swept over me.

I asked Jake to pick me up, as I didn't have my car with me. More so, I didn't like bad news delivered over the phone. It was impersonal, blunt in a way. I hoped something hadn't happened to Cassie or Bob.

Jake didn't say much when he drove, swerving, gunning the pedal. I tried not to imagine the worst that could happen. How bad could it get?

CHAPTER TWENTY-EIGHT

THE SUSPENSE WAS KILLING ME. I GROWLED AT JAKE, which wasn't my usual way of communicating. I had to get his attention.

"What happened?"

"Cassie and Bob surprised a burglar when they got home."

I gasped. They had dropped me off a short while ago.

"Did they see who it was?"

"I don't know the details."

"Anybody hurt?"

"Bob tussled with him, and they had a fight."

He pulled up the driveway, squeezing the car into a tight space. A police cruiser was parked at an angle on the road, its wheel squished against the sidewalk pavement. I supposed they could park anywhere they wanted to, seeing how they wrote their own tickets.

I followed Jake, striding as he dashed in. Whoever was here had left the kitchen drawers open like they were in such a rush, they couldn't take the time to close them. Thankfully, no glasses or dishware were smashed.

The bedrooms were another story. Cassie's room was a mess. The intruder had tossed her clothes on the floor and emptied contents of drawers on the bed. Empty drawers piled on the floor where they had been thrown. Cassie was being questioned by the police, standing with her arms folded.

I looked in my room. I hadn't packed much and didn't have a lot of stuff. My dresser drawers were rummaged and left open.

Bob's closet bedroom at the end of the hallway was untouched. He was talking to the police now as he held a towel to his face, trying to squelch the blood streaming down his nose. I heard him say the intruder had been surprised when he and Cassie walked in. At least he didn't use a knife or a gun. Bob was lucky.

I had a queasy feeling in my stomach. This was hitting close to home—it was personal now. What was the burglar searching for?

CHAPTER TWENTY-NINE

JAKE SAID HE HAD A DEADLINE TO MEET AND RUSHED back to the office. He had drafted the story on the attack on Blake, leaving out his medical condition and details about his coma.

He wanted to add a short piece on this burglary for the crime section. *Beach Beat* had the usual announcements for births, weddings, and funerals; sections on sports, upcoming events, and community and civic meetings; and want ads. They even had a section to announce awards, new jobs, and promotions. I listened with interest when Jake mentioned high school graduations were a big deal, and when the time came in May, a list of graduating senior names were published, which was a tradition. Proud parents were known to save and buy extra copies.

After Jake and the police left, I went to the kitchen and boiled some water. I hugged Cassie before gently guiding her to a chair. She sat down, her hair disheveled and body sagging. Bob still held the bloody towel over his face.

They both looked like they could use a cup of calming chamomile tea. I got out three mugs from the cupboard and tore open the box I'd bought two days ago. I dunked a tea bag in each, poured steaming water over them, and set them on the kitchen table.

"You're not hurt?" I asked Cassie.

She shook her head.

"How'd it happen?"

"We surprised the guy coming in when we did," Bob said. "He was in the hallway, headed to my room. I shouted and tackled him. He flipped me and jabbed me in the nose —hard." Bob paused to reposition the blood-soaked towel to find a clean spot, and re-applied it, flinching.

"It happened so quick," Cassie said. "Bob was momentarily stunned. The guy dashed out of here. I didn't go after him. He was a lot bigger than me. I stayed with Bob and called the police."

"Did you guys see his face?"

"No, he wore a mask. I couldn't tell what he looked like. And he wore gloves," Cassie said.

"Did you hear him speak?"

"Nope," they both said at the same time.

I squeezed Cassie's hand and gently pushed the mug toward her. "Have some hot tea. It'll calm you down." I gave Bob a mug. "You, too."

I told them Jake was submitting his story on Blake, and it would be in the paper tomorrow. The burglary would be listed in the crime section.

Cassie straightened up. "I have to call Nora, tell her what happened before she sees it in the paper tomorrow."

I had forgotten about Nora with everything happening. Cassie was right to give her a heads up.

"Guys, is anything missing?" I asked.

"The police took photos and fingerprints," Cassie said. "I told them we'd let them know after we had a chance to go over everything. They'll attach an addendum to the report. What a mess." She sighed and shook her head.

I'd have to do the same in my room. But I didn't have much stuff, and I could tell quickly if something was taken.

"Need my help?" I asked.

"No, I have to go through it myself to check for missing items." Cassie gripped the mug so tightly, the skin stretched over her knuckles. "Ugh, he didn't have to touch my bras and underwear. They're all going in the wash now. Hot water and bleach."

I jumped in. "I'm washing mine, too."

A rush of repulsion, outrage, and righteous anger surged through my veins. I thought about the stranger going through our stuff, violating our space. Who was this man, and what had he been doing here?

CHAPTER THIRTY

I DIDN'T SLEEP WELL. AFTER TOSSING AND TURNING, I finally dozed off for a short period. My throat felt dry, so I got up to get a glass of water. Jumping back in bed, I tried closing my eyes again, but my mind was racing, going full speed. I was agitated and anxious. I turned on one side, then switched to the other before falling asleep.

The loud ringing of my cell phone abruptly woke me. I fumbled and reached for it, staring at the time, cursing at the person who dared to call this early. It was seven in the morning.

"This better be good," I barked into the phone, my voice heavy and garbled with sleep.

"Eve."

I recognized Jake's voice. I rubbed my eyes and blinked.

"You *do* realize what time it is?" I said.

"I'm sorry, but I even waited before I called."

There was something in his voice. He couldn't hide it. I had a bad feeling. I sat up in bed.

"There's been a murder," Jake said.

My heart sank. I shivered. How much worse could this get?

"Who?" I croaked.

"A guy named Jeremiah."

My pulse quickened; I tightened my grip on my phone. "Jeb? The guy who found Blake's body?"

My mouth hung open.

The silence at the other end confirmed my fears.

"Where was he?" I asked.

"On the beach."

"How ... Who found him? When?" I mumbled.

"Some joggers on their early morning run at sunrise."

I leaned back on the headboard; my body had gone limp.

"You said it was *murder*," I said. I didn't blame him, but he was the messenger, and I had an urge to shake him and scream. I could understand why people say don't kill the messenger.

"Yes. They called 911. When the police came, they turned his body over. It looked like he had a ..." Jake paused.

"What?" I asked impatiently.

"He had a seashell stuffed in his mouth. His lips were stretched wide open."

I shrieked and uttered a profanity.

"He ..." I couldn't finish the sentence. Poor Jeb. Why would someone kill him? Was this murder linked to the robbery yesterday? Did it have something to do with the fact that Jeb was first at the scene at the food truck and discovered Blake? Or a coincidence with nothing to do with any of those things?

Jake was silent.

I swallowed and reached for my pencil on the nightstand. I needed it. It was all chewed up, but it was my comfort, my habit. Heck, it was what I'd always done since I had teeth. I'd gnaw my pencil until it was all covered with my teeth marks. It wasn't one pencil. It had been replaced hundreds of times over the course of my life. I needed it now. I was in shock.

CHAPTER THIRTY-ONE

I LEFT A NOTE FOR CASSIE AND BOB BEFORE I LEFT THE house. Cassie didn't finish going over her stuff last night. She was exhausted and had left her clothes in the washer. I took them out and transferred them to the dryer. Cassie was going to stay home and work on it this morning. Bob had said he'd stay with her. He wasn't going to leave her alone, not after what happened yesterday. I was glad he was here. Otherwise, I'd feel guilty leaving Cassie alone. We were a team, like we were when we were lab partners.

I headed out to meet up with Jake at the *Beach Beat* building. He had gone to the office for an unscheduled early meeting to brief his editor and the staff. A killer was loose in the community. Decisions had to be made by the paper, which remained a print-first weekly, unlike daily newspapers in large cities with website editions. They could investigate the story and have the front page lead with the murder. Jake had asked me earlier if I wanted to help out as an intern. I had, of course, agreed. He had planned to mention it to his boss and get the approval, then bring it up in the staff meeting and make the announcement. I'd be an unofficial, unpaid intern. And he'd be my mentor.

Jake had texted me a thumbs-up. I braced myself for a busy day—my first day as an intern—but nevertheless I had a job and a title, thanks to Jake. I stopped to buy a box of donuts. I didn't normally work well before I'd had my coffee and breakfast. I hoped I wouldn't let him down. There was an urgency to find the killer and the answers. A murderer was in the community, and we had a job to do.

I couldn't stop thinking about poor Jeremiah ... Jeb. What if the joggers hadn't found him? How long had he been dead? Who was the killer? Did Jeb know the killer, or did a stranger do the deed?

JAKE TOOK me to the scene of the crime and dropped me off. He had been here already and had work to do. I wanted to be left alone. It was a stretch of beach that was rather isolated. What was Jeb doing out there? Was he a runner? I didn't take him for one from my impression of him. Maybe he was killed hours earlier, late at night, and nobody found him until morning. The onlookers had dispersed by the time I got there. I strolled toward the ocean and followed the shoreline toward town. I didn't know what I was looking for, but being on foot and moving gave me something to do. I found a few sand dollars among an assortment of shells and many scattered shell fragments. One could get lucky, I supposed, and discover an amazing find early in the morning. By this time of day, the pickings were slim.

I ended up walking all the way back to town. I estimated the distance was around a couple of miles or so. I went to the food truck lot. I lingered in front of Blake's crêpe truck and circled around it. Nothing had changed.

My stomach grumbled, and I went to the burger and hot dog vendor next to Blake's truck. A different guy stood at the window. I placed an order. While I waited, I thought of another question for Larry. When the food was ready for pickup, the guy appeared.

"Larry here?" I asked.

"Nope."

"When's he coming back?"

"Who's asking?"

"Eve Sawyer, *Beach Beat*."

Oh, I liked saying it. It rolled off my tongue before I could stop. It was what Jake would say. I said it just like him.

The man raised his eyebrows. "I haven't seen you before."

"I've come by once before and talked to Larry."

He shook his head. "Larry ain't working here no more."

"But I talked to him the other day. He left?"

He paused and stared, eyeing me like he was trying to make up his mind.

"I'm new here, and Larry was friendly toward me," I said.

"Larry's gone."

It didn't make sense. I'd just met him, and now he was gone. Why didn't he stay on the job?

"I'd like to talk to him. Can you ask him to call me?"

"I ain't promising anything."

"Please, it's important." I reached for my pen and wrote down my contact information. "You can reach me here."

He folded the slip of paper and tucked it in his apron pocket.

"By the way," he added. "Larry wanted to leave. He made it sound like he got a better offer somewhere else. I didn't bother to ask."

I turned to leave, but a question popped in my mind. I spun around.

"Have you seen a man in a suit lurking here?"

CHAPTER THIRTY-TWO

BLAKE'S APARTMENT WAS A SHORT WALK FROM THE FOOD truck. It was away from the hustle and bustle of Central Avenue. Tall, majestic oak and magnolia trees shaded the house and lawn, their canopies providing a welcome relief from the relentless sun. I stood in the shade, face uplifted, catching a breeze stirring the leaves with a gentle rustling. It was quiet, peaceful … until a cat darted across my path. A black and white cat.

It was a friendly little bugger and rubbed my legs. I stooped to pet it. A female.

I picked her up to have a better look at her cute tuxedo face.

"And who might you be?" I asked, scratching behind her ear. She yawned and nuzzled her face in my cupped hand, sniffing the new scent.

I heard the screen door slam on the first floor of the house, and a woman bellowed across the yard. She was dressed in a shapeless, thin cotton shift and wearing house slippers.

"Thelma!" she screeched.

"Is this your cat?" I said, even though it was rather obvious when I brought the cat to her.

"My Thelma got out again." She sprang into action as another cat, an orange tabby, slipped out. "And that's Kika."

The flabby skin under her arms swung as she reached for the cat. I surrendered Thelma and watched as she smothered the feline with kisses and baby talk. She finally released it inside the house, before shutting the screen door and turning around to me. I doubt she left the house much, from the way she was dressed.

"And who might you be, young lady?"

I didn't get a thanks, but her tone was friendly. I decided to be straight. I sensed a shrewdness, making it hard for anyone to get past her BS radar.

"I'm Eve Sawyer," I said, holding out my hand.

She scrutinized me. "You're new around here?"

"I'm actually on vacation, visiting my friend Cassie."

She frowned.

"I, um … I'm an intern at *Beach Beat*."

I detected a flicker of interest or curiosity when I mentioned the paper. Was she a devout reader of the local weekly?

"You nosing around for a story?"

"As a matter of fact, I was hoping to talk to you today." By her expression, I could tell this caught her by surprise. "Are you Blake Conway's landlady?"

"The police have already questioned me," she said.

"I'm working with Jake Thorne on a story. May I ask a few questions?"

I saw the hesitation in her eyes for a brief moment. She didn't waver long.

"What do you want to know?"

"A man named Jeremiah was murdered early this morning, or maybe late last night," I said.

She gasped, putting her hand over her mouth.

"I understand he was a long-time resident here in town, known for his trademark orange T-shirt."

"Yes, he was." She nodded.

"Has he ever come around here to see Blake? I understand Jeb was a friend of his."

She grunted. Fluffed her hair. "Well now, I believe the two of them have hung out here."

"Did you notice anything out of the ordinary?"

"Naw. Those two were quiet."

I chewed on my lip while I thought about my next question.

"Ma'am, what is your name?"

"You can call me Mrs. Berry."

"Well, Mrs. Berry," I said, leaning toward her. "Maybe you and I can stop whoever is running around killing folks here."

The roll of her eyes told me she *hadn't* thought of it that way.

"Do you think . . . ?" she said.

I nodded vigorously. "Yes, I do. And you know whoever did it—well, he or she may be coming around here next."

One hand flew to her chest and gripped the thin

cotton shift, pulling it in a clump. "You figure they'll be coming here?"

Damn right, I did, but I softened it. "We ought to think this through. You don't have all the information. Here's what I think happened. Whoever attacked Blake left him for dead or was interrupted. Then Blake's friend's home was burglarized. Then Jeb, another friend of Blake's, was discovered dead this morning on the beach." I paused. "Don't you see? The only connection to all of these people is Blake."

Mrs. Berry's mouth dropped open. I thought she'd throw her two cents in, but she was speechless.

"Blake," she murmured, shaking her head.

"Now, Mrs. Berry, I want you to try and remember. Do you recall anything else Blake has said? Have you seen anyone else coming to see him?"

Mrs. Berry puckered her lips and frowned. "Now that you're asking, there was someone else."

"Who?"

"This girl, she's come over."

"What's her name?"

"He didn't exactly introduce her. But I recognized her. She's Nora's granddaughter."

I laughed. "She's Cassie, the friend I'm staying with."

She smiled. "Yes, Cassie."

I cleared my throat. "Ma'am, have you seen a man in a suit here?"

She shook her head, "Can't say I have. Although …"

"Yes?"

"Although, Blake swung by here once, and he ran into his apartment like he was in a hurry and kept the engine running. Someone was sitting in the passenger side front seat."

I sucked in my breath. "Who did you see?"

"Couldn't tell for sure, but it was a female. She had sunglasses on, and her hair was pulled back. Then Blake got back in the car and drove off in a hurry."

I sighed, my thoughts turning to him. "Cassie and I —we went to the hospital to see Blake."

"How is he?"

"He's still in a coma."

"We've been praying for him," Mrs. Berry said. "Me and my husband, and the ladies' circle at the church."

❧

THE POLICE QUESTIONED Cassie again in the morning. Was Cassie their prime suspect now? Why did Blake call her that night? What did Cassie know?

Could my intuition or sixth sense about Cassie be wrong?

CHAPTER THIRTY-THREE

I WALKED BACK TO MY CAR AT THE NEWSPAPER OFFICE. I wanted to laugh and cry. One or the other, or both. I mean, how absurd could this get? My breadcrumbs were fewer and fewer and harder to come by. They were leading me on a road to nowhere. This wasn't a situation where I could make lemonade out of it. I could release my tears, spilling them in sheer despair and deeper frustration. I was running into a dead end. Laugh or cry ... it wasn't going to change the facts.

I buried my head in my hands. Blake was in the hospital, and Jeremiah was dead. Were the two related? Had someone tried to kill him because he knew something about Blake?

I had to figure it out. Clear my mind.

My phone buzzed. I'd put it on silent, and it vibrated with an incoming call.

I didn't recognize the number. "Hello," I said cautiously.

"I heard you were looking for me," a man's voice said.

I didn't recognize the unfamiliar voice. "I think you have the wrong number."

"It's me, Larry."

"Larry, the hot dog and burger guy?" My voice rose slightly higher.

"Yes, you'd left me a message, and I'm calling you back."

"I went by your food truck, but the guy said you were no longer working there."

"I left."

"Where are you? Can we meet?" My heart thumped, beating against my chest. I squeezed the phone, tightening my fingers.

"There's a park near town. You can map it on your phone. Meet me there. I'll be sitting on a bench near the statue of the water boy."

My hands shook. I barely knew Larry. He wanted to meet me in the park? Did he feel safer there?

I clicked on the map icon on my cell and typed "park" in the search bar. It popped up a short distance away, about five miles. I powered up the car engine and stepped on the gas pedal.

I drove to the park. Its sign stood back and was unobtrusive. I veered off the paved road, following the winding, graveled one inside the park to the parking lot. One other vehicle was there, which I guessed had to be Larry's. It was a small park. It was easy to spot the bronze statue of a boy in the clearing. Larry was there, sitting on the bench. It was quiet, out of the way, and from where he sat, it was a good vantage point, easy to spot other visitors.

Larry was dressed nicely and looked different without an apron. Gone was his easygoing, customer-service smile. Nervously, his eyes flitted around.

"Hey, this is a quaint place," I said. I made a mental note to explore this place before my time ended here, if I had time left.

"Anyone follow you here?"

I wasn't particularly on alert, but I was careful and would've noticed if anyone had followed me. "Nope. So what happened, you quit or something?"

"I started a fight with the owner, then we both said at once, 'I quit' and 'You're fired.' Makes no difference to me, got what I wanted."

I waited, curious to see where this was going.

He said, "Listen, I thought about our conversation—"

"Did you know Jeb was murdered?"

He tapped his foot, shaking his legs, and nodded. I thought his eyes twitched. "I may be next."

My heart skipped a beat. Was he in danger now after Jeb's death?

"Is that why you quit?"

He sighed. "When Blake was attacked, I got worried."

I stuttered. "But ... why would someone come after you?"

Larry cupped his face, but he didn't answer my question.

"Have you noticed anything odd?"

"There's a guy. He'd been watching me. I should say us, me and Blake. I noticed him first, and I mentioned it to Blake."

"Did he know the guy?"

"Blake said he'd never laid eyes on him before. The guy wore a suit. He'd be there for hours, watching everyone who came up to our food trucks. You know … watching Jeb." Larry dropped to a whisper. His eyes darted, looking around, scanning across the landscape into the distance. "See the church steeple and the tombstones?" he said.

"Where?"

"On the hilltop. Do you see it?"

I nodded. The sky above was crisp blue, no fluffy clouds in sight. Other than the distant chirping of birds, it was just us talking. Not another living soul around.

CHAPTER THIRTY-FOUR

"I THOUGHT I SAW SOMEONE UP THERE," LARRY SAID quietly. "I'm paranoid. The man in the suit. He gave me the willies."

"Did you see what car he drove?"

"A dark green, late model sedan."

"Did he talk to you?"

"No. When Blake closed shop, he looked harried, and his jaw was clenched."

"Not good, huh?"

He shuddered.

"I don't know why you'd mentioned the tombstones, but you're spooking me out with all this talk about the man in the suit."

I wanted to shake him. I was so infuriated. Here I was trying to help the man, meeting him in an isolated place like this, and for what? I was flabbergasted. I counted to three before I finally opened my mouth. I held back the curses.

"You do realize you asked me to meet you out

here?" I said. "If you don't have anything to tell me, I'm leaving." I gathered my things.

"He's still here," Larry said.

"Who, the man in the suit?"

"Yeah."

"How do you know?"

"A stroke of luck. I went by the market one night. I saw his car parked outside. I recognized the color, and I thought it might be his, but I couldn't be sure. I stayed outside and waited for him to come out."

I held my breath.

"I didn't have long to wait. He carried a bag of groceries and a six-pack."

"Was he still dressed in a suit?"

Larry nodded and pointed his finger. Bingo.

"And then what happened?"

"I followed him home."

My mind was processing this information. If Larry was right about this man in the suit, we'd better find him—fast.

"What is the address?"

"I'll do one better. I'll take you there."

I stared at him. So he wasn't running from this man, but he was going to see him? Was Larry telling the truth? There was one way to find out.

"What are you waiting for? Let's go see Mr. Suit," I said.

CHAPTER THIRTY-FIVE

LARRY PULLED UP IN FRONT OF A HOUSE. A FAMILIAR house. It was Sandy Dayne's place.

The pieces were starting to come together. Sandy Dayne had spoken out at the town hall meeting, opposing the plastics ban ordinance Blake had worked on. Then Blake was attacked in his food truck and was now in a coma. Jeb was next, and he paid with his life. Larry had quit his job to bolt. He thought he'd be the next one. The common thread was Blake and the plastics ban. Both Jeb and Larry had helped him distribute flyers and knock on doors. The three of them together. All three were committed and helping Blake. One had been attacked, another killed, and the third might be next. Find Mr. Suit, and the case was solved, right? Could it be that simple? Or had this man disappeared?

I scanned the driveway, carport, and the street for the dark green sedan. I was ready to interview him if we could catch him. I pulled out my pencil, now halfway gnawed with bite marks. I stuck it back in my mouth and chomped like a mad woman.

We sat there and scoped out the place. Larry got out of the car. I sprinted after him, my eyes on alert. It didn't look like anyone was home. The windows were dark, and the house was quiet. Larry crept closer and peeked inside the front door's glass pane. He made his way around the house, testing windows and the back door, but they were locked.

I was intrigued by Mr. Suit, a suspected killer on the loose. My adrenaline level surged. My heartbeat quickened.

The shrill chime programmed to Jake's number on my cell sounded. I jabbed my finger on the screen to take the call.

"Jake," I whispered while I made my way around to the backyard.

"Why are you acting weird?"

"Remember Sandy Dayne, the guy we were looking for? Well, I'm at his house, but it looks like he's not at home."

"What are you doing there?"

"Larry says he may be the killer."

"Who says?"

"Larry from the burger food truck," I said. "Well, he used to work there. He's been tracking Mr. Suit."

"Who's Mr. Suit?"

"Well, that's what I call him, the man Larry referred to as the man in the suit. He's been watching Blake and him, freaking Larry out."

"I know where you are," Jake said. "I'll be right there."

CHAPTER THIRTY-SIX

When Jake arrived, I introduced Larry, and he brought Jake up to speed on what he knew. I wanted him to hear it firsthand. Jake's face paled as he listened. When Larry finished speaking, Jake threw a thanks as he rushed toward his car, with me in tow.

"Jump in," Jake said, holding the car door open.

I threw Larry my car keys and told him I'd make arrangements for someone to pick it up.

I didn't hesitate, sliding in the front passenger seat.

"Where're we going?" I asked.

"To the capital," Jake said. I could tell we were heading northwest, which meant it would take about an hour-and-a-half to reach it.

Jake explained he had tracked Sandy Dayne down. But he didn't call ahead and request an interview to give him a heads-up. Said this was better, catching him by surprise.

I called Bob to let him know where I was going and

to ask about Cassie. I gave him Larry's number and asked Bob to pick up my car.

Jake was quiet during my brief call.

We headed inland, veering away from the coastal highway, leaving the beach behind. I stared out the window, chewing my bottom lip. My swimsuit had barely gotten wet, and I'd dipped in the Atlantic Ocean twice. This vacation had turned out to be anything but fun and sun. I was peeved, out of sorts, and annoyed at the world. Feeling mighty sorry for myself.

I didn't want to talk. I turned up the AC. The oppressive humidity outside sucked my energy; I felt myself dragging. My sweat had turned sticky with the heavy, moisture-laden air. The cool air inside was a reprieve.

"Thirsty?" Jake asked.

"I could do with a drink."

"Back seat, in the cooler. Take your pick."

"You came prepared," I said, smiling as I reached behind and rummaged in the container. Bottled water. What the heck? Was this his idea of a selection? They all looked the same. I reached to the bottom and scooped out a bottle, shaking the moisture from it. I squinted to examine the fine print on the label—artesian water—relieved it wasn't bottled tap water from a municipal source. Twisting the cap, I took a long sip, enjoying the refreshing, clean taste, devoid of the metallic tang I detested. I raised the clear bottle up and smacked my lips.

"It's that good, huh?" Jake grinned. "You sure know how to pick winners."

I laughed. He sure made it easy. "Want one?"

Jake shook his head. "It's all yours," he said, pointing to the drink holder in the center console.

I hadn't seen much humor coming from Jake—until now. I liked it. I made a mental note, wiping away the pinched expression as my irritable mood faded. My tense muscles relaxed, and I slumped down, curving into the passenger seat and letting my head sink onto the headrest.

This guy doesn't even know me, yet he can take the edge off. Yes, I could be bitchy, moody, and unpleasant to be around. It wasn't limited to once a month, either. Most people didn't know how to handle me, so they distanced themselves and left me alone. Jake wasn't like all the others.

CHAPTER THIRTY-SEVEN

My nerves couldn't handle speeding or erratic movements. I didn't have to worry. Jake was a good driver.

"I want to tell you more about Blake," Jake said, throwing me a quick glance.

"Oh yeah, what?"

"He's an indefatigable worker, focused on succeeding, driving himself relentlessly, even foregoing sleep and food. He has a wide range of interests and comes up with unique ideas. Runs with them. He has bundles of creative energy. Doesn't take no for an answer. Sees everything as a challenge. He isn't afraid to start at the bottom."

"How did he end up here, doing the crêpe thing?"

"Blake is passionate about the environment, sustainable local farming, organic foods, the farm-to-table sort of thing. And there's an explosion of interest in food trucks. So this stint—his food truck business—is a natural evolution. Blake tests new ideas and creates new foods and menus, bringing a freshness to the competitive food truck industry. If he succeeds in crêpes, he wants to expand to other cities and states."

"What new ideas or offerings does he have?"

"He offers gluten-free and vegan crêpes, and farm-fresh, organic ingredients. He incorporates seasonal fruits and local produce, which can vary by the region. Crêpes are versatile. Sweet or savory. Plain or gourmet. Main meal or dessert. Countless other combinations. It works well with the kitchen set-up in the truck. It's easy to make this a popular offering for food truck customers."

I got excited. "So he can take a food truck to any city or state and incorporate aspects of local foods, produce, and cuisine into the crêpes, as well as the language and culture in the menu. It's brilliant."

"Yes, and the concept he's seized on makes sense business-wise and compliments his creative side, with room to grow and expand. Who knows, it could even be international. He can easily adapt to regional tastes and seasonal foods, and vary the menu. There are staples, of course, like egg crêpes for breakfast or lunch, or sweet snacks."

"Sweet crêpes?" I asked.

"Filled and topped with a variety of berries like strawberries, blueberries, blackberries; fresh fruit like apples, bananas, peaches, pears; or other dessert fillings and toppings. He started with strawberry crêpes, but the plan was to offer more selections."

"You're making me hungry," I said. "So where did Blake learn how to make crêpes?"

"He went to crêpe school."

"You're joking. Where?"

"Blake wanted to be authentic, so he went to Brittany to train to be a crêpe chef and to visit as many crêperies as he could."

"How delightful," I said, making a mental note, adding adorable French crêperies to my travel wish list.

"Hey, while we're here, I'd like to interview Blake's sister," Jake said.

"She lives here?"

"Lives and works here."

I sat up, adjusting the seat belt. My ears perked up. "Did you call her?"

Jake patted his pocket. "I got her number here."

"Will she see us?"

"I don't see why not. But we'll find out soon enough."

My heartbeat raced. I couldn't wait to meet Blake's sister. Ask her questions.

❧

SHE AGREED to meet Jake for an interview. It was after six, and she was still at work, so we went to her office. The Thirst company was located in a sleek, shiny, tall building at a prime downtown location. We signed in at the front lobby and stepped in the elevator.

I followed Jake as he made his way through cubicles and a row of walled offices. Her office was at the end.

A female voice said, "Come in," when he knocked.

The office was spacious, but sparsely decorated. A small glass conference table with four chairs was at one end of the room, close to the door. A desk was at the other side of the room. She was sitting in front of the computer with her back to us, her brunette hair loosely coiled in a bun, wearing a tailored, pink pants suit.

Jake cleared his throat. At the sound, she swirled around, swinging the diamond drop earrings dangling from a beautiful heart-shaped face, a ready smile on her lips.

I gasped.

CHAPTER THIRTY-EIGHT

EVEN WITH HER MAKEUP ON AND TAILORED SUIT, SHE looked familiar. It took me a second to place her, as I scanned my memory. Yes, I was right.

"Kaitlyn." The word flew out of my mouth. She was the woman wearing a pair of beat-up jeans in the crowd when I bumped into her in front of Blake's food truck.

Her smile stopped. Her dark brown eyes widening at the sight of me confirmed it.

Jake stepped in. "Jake Thorne, *Beach Beat,* and this is my new intern, Eve Sawyer."

"We met at Blake's food truck," I said in the most friendly voice I could use. "I—I didn't realize you were Blake's sister."

Kaitlyn's eyes flickered, cool to match her glare. She gestured to the two seats across from her desk. "Have a seat."

She didn't offer us a drink, although water bottles

sat on the stainless steel counter. I sensed she wanted to get rid of us, fast.

"Is this about Blake? Did he wake up?" Kaitlyn said.

Jake sighed, barely perceptible. "Blake is still in a coma and fighting for his life. We'd like to ask you a few questions. Can you tell us anything about who may have done this?" Jake said.

She toyed with a paper clip, prodding it with an expensive, glossy pen. "He moved, and we lost touch for a while after college. I'm not the best person to ask about this."

"When did you first go see him at Lolly Beach?" Jake asked.

She hesitated. Maybe Kaitlyn realized she had to explain why she was there. Did she have a chance to see Blake before the morning he was assaulted? Why didn't Kaitlyn tell me she was Blake's sister? Was she in shock? In denial? I was busy thinking of answers, and I didn't realize she'd started speaking.

"Two days before."

"Did he mention anyone who may be trying to harm him?"

"He didn't mention anyone specifically. I do believe he may have had suspicions."

I leaned forward. This could be important.

"What makes you say that?" Jake asked.

"The way he looked around, when we were talking, and twiddled his thumb and cracked his fingers, like he used to do when he was a child."

"Did you visit Blake in the hospital?"

"Of course."

"When did you return?"

"Last night. I rushed back to meet a deadline. He was still in a coma when I left. The hospital will let me know if his condition changes."

Jake shifted in his seat and continued his questioning.

"You live here, work here?"

She nodded.

"Isn't it a coincidence that you happened to be there, an hour-and-a-half's drive away, on the day Blake was attacked?"

Kaitlyn pursed her lips, squeezing a tight smile, which didn't reach her eyes.

"Why did you go to see him?" Jake persisted.

"He called me, asked for my help."

"Help with what?"

"He was working on a new plastics ban ordinance and wanted my opinion … you know, from someone in the industry he could trust."

"Couldn't you have told him over the phone?" Jake asked.

She blinked, pausing as if to carefully word her next sentence. "He wanted something from me, in person."

"You went to see him the day of his attack?"

"No, it was two days before."

"What did you give him?"

"Information he wanted."

"Can you share it with us?"

"I'm afraid not."

"Tell me about your relationship. Did you two get along? Have fights?"

"We've had our ups and downs." She cleared her throat. "We had a falling out in college. He didn't talk to me for years."

"When you met with him a few days ago, did you make amends?"

She nodded. "In the end, we did. We loved each other and would do anything for one other."

CHAPTER THIRTY-NINE

We left Kaitlyn's office and scurried to our next interview.

Sandy Dayne's place turned out to be in a nice, gentrified area. The district contained older buildings, which had been renovated.

Jake said it always worked to play a damsel in distress. Who wouldn't be a gentleman in that situation? We didn't have a chance to rehearse. A bald, pudgy man wearing glasses sauntered to the door and entered the building code on the keypad. I went into action, pretending I'd twisted an ankle while Jake was supporting me and yelling to the man.

"Hold the door, please."

The man was a gentleman, holding the building door for us. We entered the elevator together. He pushed the number three and asked us, "What floor?"

When Jake answered, he hit the top button for us.

We had no trouble finding the penthouse. On the second knock, a handsome, middle-aged man answered the door. I guessed his age to be in the forties. He wasn't dressed in a suit, but he looked distinguished, his salt-and-pepper hair impeccably trimmed. He was dressed casually, but even in his pressed shirt and pants, he had a dignified presence.

Jake whipped out his ID and introduced us. "Jake Thorne, *Beach Beat,* and Eve Sawyer."

The man's eyebrows lifted when he peered at Jake's photo and press credentials.

"We would like to speak to Sandy Dayne. Are you him?" Jake asked.

"What's this about?" The man appeared to be genuinely perplexed.

"We are looking for a Sandy Dayne who was at Lolly Beach and possibly a suspect in an attack," Jake said.

"I'm Sandy Dayne, but I'm afraid you've confused me with someone else. Care to explain?" He moved back, opening the door wider, and gestured to the living room. "Please come in."

Entering the expansive dwelling, my jaw dropped open. I stretched my neck to view the height of the ceiling and swirled around to catch the magnificent skyline views from the floor-to-ceiling windows. Speechless, I managed to catch Jake's eye. He winked, putting me at ease and grounding me.

I was sure I wasn't the first or only one to be impressed.

"Cool place," I managed to mumble. Heck, I'd whistle, too.

Sandy Dayne paraded around the room, pointing

out buildings of note, historic markers, and landscapes. As soon as the tour finished, we got down to business. Sandy agreed to be interviewed. We sat on the living room couch.

"Mr. Dayne, did you attend the Lolly Beach town council meeting last week on the plastics ban ordinance?" Jake said.

"No," Sandy said.

"Have you visited Lolly Beach within the last month?"

Sandy shook his head.

"What is your line of work?"

"I'm an industry consultant."

"Can you be more specific?"

"I work with the beverage industry."

"Do you know Blake Conway?"

Up to this point, Sandy had answered quickly and without hesitation. At the mention of Blake, he blanched.

"Blake Conway ring a bell?" Jake prodded.

Sandy gave a slight nod.

"Were you aware Blake was attacked and hospitalized?"

"I heard it on the news."

Now we were getting somewhere.

"How do you know Blake and when did you meet?"

Sandy shifted in the plush leather seat. "I make it my business to know the rising stars. Blake was named Young Entrepreneur of the Year, and I made sure he was introduced to me."

He got up to make himself a drink, adding ice cubes. "You want one?"

We both shook our heads. I never touched alcohol. Not because I was a prude, but it did things to me. I'd tried it before. It was good to know Jake didn't drink when he was on the job. Less chance of it tampering with his senses.

"Did you do business with Blake?"

"He can't afford me." Sandy threw back his head and laughed heartily.

CHAPTER FORTY

I WAS STILL REELING FROM SANDY'S RAUCOUS LAUGHTER, its echoes reverberating as we left his place. I ducked my head, scurrying out of the building and down the street, running ahead of Jake.

As it turned out, Sandy Dayne was telling the truth. He did know Blake Conway, but he wasn't at the town council meeting speaking out against the plastics ban ordinance. He hadn't been to the beach, and he wasn't anywhere near it. Sandy had the goods to prove it. Airline tickets and charges for his rental car.

I let out a huge sigh when we reached Jake's car. I was running on adrenaline, expecting a big break in the case, a scoop. But we had nothing on Sandy.

My hand gripped the door handle, ready to pull it open at the click of the remote. I sank in the passenger seat and put on my seat belt as Jake cranked the engine and put it in gear, merging into the traffic.

I checked my cell. Cassie had left me a voicemail. Now what?

"Hey, Cassie," I said when she answered.

"Wh—where are you now?" Her voice cracked.

"I'm with Jake. We're in the city, heading back." I kept my voice calm and soothing. Cassie had been through so much. "Hey, I'll be there as soon as I can. I'll text you when I'm close."

She let out a quiet exhale.

"How are you?" I asked. I refused to give up hope, and I couldn't let Cassie down.

My ears caught a whimper and sounds of soft crying.

"I'm sorry, I wish I could give you a hug." I waited, giving Cassie as much time as she needed.

"We need to talk," Cassie finally said.

CHAPTER FORTY-ONE

JAKE DROVE US BACK TO THE BEACH. RIGHT THROUGH AN ominous summer thunderstorm. The sky darkened as the heavy clouds drew a curtain over the remains of the daylight. Bursts of lightning flashed, lighting up the sky momentarily.

Rain pelted the windshield, splashing and producing streams faster than the wipers could brush aside. The intense drumming of the rain and the rhythmic squish of the windshield wipers replaced our conversation. Jake gripped the wheel, eyes focused on the road through the foggy windshield. I didn't break his concentration.

It took forever, but I made it home.

"Thanks, Jake. See you tomorrow," I said, opening the car door. Drops of rain covered my bare arms and legs, and the wetness soaked through my thin cotton top and dampened my hair. I dashed across the driveway.

Cassie was expecting me and opened the door.

I smiled, pointing to my wet clothes. "The hug will have to wait."

"I'll make us some tea while you change," Cassie said, moving toward the kitchen.

Tea sounded good. I quickly wiped down with a dry towel and changed into my favorite pair of comfy jeans and a clean T-shirt.

I joined Cassie at the table, where she placed two piping hot mugs of tea. I sipped and closed my eyes as the warm liquid glided down my throat. I sighed. My happy sigh. When I glanced at Cassie, she was grinning.

"Now, this is perfect." I looked around. "Where's Bob?"

"He went to bed early. Said to tell you he got your car and something about a headache."

It was late—the tortuous drive back took longer than I'd expected.

"Am I keeping you up?" I asked.

"No, I can't sleep. Haven't been able to lately."

I paused to take another sip. "Cassie, you said you wanted to talk."

"It's been crazy, you know." Her voice dropped and trembled as she looked away.

I reached out, put my hand over hers, and gave a gentle squeeze. "Yes, I know." I had questions I wanted to ask. About Blake. And her. But before I did, I told Cassie about my trip to see Kaitlyn Conway and Sandy Dayne. I noticed a faint flush in Cassie's cheeks when I mentioned Blake's sister.

"Did you ever meet his sister?"

"No, but he's talked about her."

"What did he say?"

"They were once close, but then they didn't speak for years."

"Did he tell you why?"

She shook her head.

I saw the way Cassie acted after Blake was attacked.

"Tell me what's going on with you and Blake." I said, speaking softly.

She shook her head.

"You have feelings for him."

"Yes."

"You're close?"

"We were growing closer. When Blake first arrived, I was one of his initial customers. I was curious about his crêpes, and he talked me into one. He said if I didn't like it, he would refund my money. Said he'd bet on it. And we did. Wager a bet."

"So what if you liked it? What did he bet?"

"He said, since I've lived here all my life, I knew all the places. So if he won, then I'd have to show him around and take him to all the non-tourist spots."

"So he won the bet?"

Cassie laughed—the kind of laugh I loved from the old Cassie I missed.

CHAPTER FORTY-TWO

THE NEXT DAY, JAKE AND I SHOWED SANDY DAYNE'S picture, which he'd snapped on his phone, to Big Ralph, the neighbor. He didn't recognize him. Nor did Larry. Sandy's story checked out. He wasn't here.

Jake went through the files from the town council meeting and rummaged for photos. He found the picture he was looking for—the man in the suit, taken when he was speaking. Jake gave it to Perry at the police station. They ran his face through the system and got a match—a lowlife thief with a record of petty crimes and robberies. They tracked him down. When the police interrogated the man, Tony Moore, he admitted to burglarizing Cassie's place after prolonged and intense questioning. He didn't have a name and couldn't put a face to the person who had hired him—said he was paid in cash, left at a cash drop. He used a burner phone, and the caller's voice had been disguised. He'd followed the directions given, down to the details of wearing a suit, watching Blake, writing down Sandy Dayne's name at the town council meeting, and donning a mask for the burglary.

Larry and Big Ralph recognized the suit right away when Jake showed them the picture. I was bummed out with Larry because he'd never mentioned one important detail about the suit. Couldn't he tell the difference between a nice suit and a cheap one? I mean, he could have said the man in the cheap suit. But I didn't stay mad at Larry for long, and we joked about his nonexistent fashion sense.

Jake and I talked. We discussed Tony Moore in detail, piecing together all we knew.

"We know the real Sandy Dayne wasn't at the meeting," I said. "And Tony Moore confessed to the burglary. But what I don't get is why he was told to write down Sandy Dayne's name when he spoke at the public meeting."

"Was it to throw suspicion on Sandy?" Jake asked.

"It's logical. Sandy's a consultant to the industry manufacturing the same plastics that Blake was trying to ban on the beach."

"So whoever did this had to know the real Sandy Dayne or his reputation and work as a consultant in the industry."

"Could be someone related to the plastics industry or even a provocateur to muddy things up?" I surmised.

"Or someone who wanted Sandy on the record opposing the ban," Jake said.

"They could have easily found his name searching the internet."

“Right.”

This was where I took out my pencil and chewed on it. I had brought a new one, since the old one was covered with teeth marks. What about poor Jeb? Did his death have anything to do with Blake, or was it a coincidence? What was I missing here?

CHAPTER FORTY-THREE

JAKE THREW ME A SMILE. "I KNOW EXACTLY WHAT YOU need."

I stopped chewing on my pencil and frowned. Couldn't he see I was busy?

"C'mon. Let's go take a walk down the street." Jake gave me a gentle shove out the door.

"I don't see why we have to go anywhere." I pushed my lower lip out and stalled.

"You'll see in a minute."

The rush of hot air was a welcome change from the air-conditioned newspaper office. I squinted in the bright sunlight before I hurried after him. Jake marched right over to a shaved ice cart and ordered two snow cones.

"What flavor would you like?" he asked.

I happened to love snow cones in the summertime. "Watermelon," I blurted out.

"Make it two," he told the vendor.

"How did you know?" I asked.

Jake winked as he handed me a paper cone overfilled with shaved ice and topped with a generous drizzle of pink watermelon syrup soaked all the way through.

The snow cone was every bit as good as it looked. I was a happy camper.

It was a pretty day. I thought of Cassie. I wanted to get her something to cheer her up. I chewed and crunched as we strolled on the sidewalk down the one main road in town, keeping an eye on the window displays.

"Give me a sec," I said, stopping in front of a beach gift store.

"What are you doing?" Jake asked as he followed me inside the store.

"Getting a gift for Cassie."

I headed toward the jewelry counter and looked over the selection. My eyes caught sight of a pair of baby blue sea-glass earrings in sterling silver. They were stylish and stunning. I quickly made the purchase.

Jake had wandered across the room to look at beach accessories, shells, and shell items. I made my way there, stopping to look them over, reminding myself to collect shells before my time was up at the beach.

"Jake, see anything you want?"

"Not yet."

"I got a little something for Cassie. Thought she might like it. She's been going through some rough times."

"I'm sure she'll appreciate whatever you got her."

The display of seashells drew my interest. There

were all kinds, mostly small and medium sizes. A variety of conch shells and a starfish.

"You collect them?" I asked.

"I used to. They get picked over by the early risers."

"Yeah, especially the pretty ones."

"So what's your favorite?" Jake asked.

"The conch shells. The almost translucent ones."

"I've found some interesting ones."

"Like what?"

"A horseshoe crab."

"That's not exactly the shell of a dead creature," I said.

"Right. It's the exoskeleton a living horseshoe crab sheds as it molts."

I picked up a bonnet polished shell, running a finger over its texture. I placed the opening to my ear.

"Can you hear the ocean?" Jake asked.

I held a finger to my lips and nodded, smiling.

"Ready to go?" Jake asked.

He gently steered me toward the door. I clutched the purchase in my hand and turned around, bumping into Jake.

"What's wrong?"

"Hey Jake, did you say Jeb was killed with a seashell in his mouth?"

"It was stuffed in his mouth."

"Did you see a picture of it?"

"No."

I picked up a random shell, a Strawberry Trochus. "Was it this one? Or an Atlantic Whelk? Or another one? How large was it?" I tried to imagine it stuffed in Jeb's mouth.

"So you want to know exactly what kind of shell?

"Yup. Can you find out?"

Jake frowned, ruffling a hand over his hair. "I can ask my police contact about it."

CHAPTER FORTY-FOUR

I WALKED BACK TO CASSIE'S HOUSE. IT WAS SUCH A gorgeous day to be outside, and I wanted some time alone to think. I had the package with the gift wrapped inside.

Bob was home and in the kitchen when I opened the door. He had finished rinsing the dishes and was in the process of stacking them in the dishwasher.

"How's your day going?" he said.

"Beautiful," I said, smiling broadly. "You should go enjoy the day."

"I'm going to make a run to the market. You want anything?"

"Nope, I'm good. How's Cassie doing today?"

"She slept in, and we had a late breakfast. Cassie should be out any minute."

I plopped down on the chair and leaned my elbows on the table.

"Were you planning to see Blake again today?" I asked.

"Maybe later, we saw him yesterday."

"How is he?"

"He's still in a coma, but holding steady."

"Have you been able to go in?"

"No, but Cassie has been talking to him outside the open door. She's visited Blake every day."

"Hey, did I hear my name mentioned?" Cassie said, smiling as she appeared with damp hair, looking like she'd just showered.

I laughed.

"You're in good spirits today," I said, tapping the chair next to me. "Come sit down. I have news for both of you."

"About the burglary?" Cassie asked.

I nodded. I had mentioned the trip to Cassie last night, but I added more details and brought them both up to speed on the trip Jake and I took to the city, our meeting with Blake's sister and Sandy Dayne, and also about Tony Moore.

"So the police have this man?" Cassie asked.

"Yes." I touched her arm reassuringly. "You can rest easy now."

I took out the gift box and slid it across the table.

Cassie squealed. "For me?"

I grinned.

Cassie opened the box, and a gasp of delight escaped. She picked up the earrings and put them on right away. She shook her head, laughing as they twirled.

A grunt came from Bob's direction, and I turned around to see him nod.

It was almost like old times again, the three of us.

CHAPTER FORTY-FIVE

My cell phone rang. It was Jake calling.

"Hey, what's up?"

"I've got a tip for you," Jake said, rushing his words.

"The seashell?"

"When they picked up the shell, they weren't sure what it was. Perry said they perused the books and called a collector to identify it."

My intuition had alerted me, and it was rarely wrong. I wriggled in my chair and wished Jake would hurry up.

"Okay, you got a name?"

"It's not to be shared."

"They wouldn't tell you?" I sighed, letting out a long breath.

"No, but I understand it wasn't a common shell. As a matter of fact, nobody had seen anything like it around here. I'm guessing it's not indigenous to this area."

"Can you describe it?"

"It's light tan and shaped like a conch. And it's large."

"What was it doing in his mouth? You suppose it might be the murder weapon?" I asked.

"Could be."

❧

I RAN out the door and drove to town, my foot on the gas, going over the speed limit. I swerved into the first parking space available and parked, heading straight for the beach gift shop. Inside, I strode to the collection of seashells and searched for a shell matching Jake's description. On the counter was a shell identification guide. It looked like the abbreviated version of a catalog, with the more common shells listed. I didn't know the names of the shells, but I was familiar with them.

Oblivious to my surroundings, I was bent over, my nose inches from the counter, viewing the shells. Then I sensed someone close.

"May I help you?"

I looked up to see a middle-aged woman with a rose tattooed on her arm. It wasn't the young clerk from earlier.

"You collect and clean these shells?"

She gave me a practiced look, one I bet she reserved for tourists.

"Oh, no," she said with a raised eyebrow. "We can order shells for you. You looking for any in particular?"

I went straight to the point. "What's the largest shell you have?"

"Well, what you see is what we have. I don't keep an inventory in the back."

"I'm looking for a light tan, conch-like shell. And it's large," I said. "But I don't see one here."

"Can you be more specific?"

"It's probably not local to this area. Have you sold anything like what I described recently?"

She frowned, shaking her head. "I don't believe I have, but let me check with my assistant."

"Hey, Leslie," she called out.

A girl with long, straggly blonde hair appeared from behind the curtain. I recognized her as the clerk who wrapped Cassie's earrings for me. She didn't look much older than sixteen, with the awkward shyness of a teenager on the cusp of adulthood.

"Oh, hi," she said, smiling.

"Do you remember selling a rather large conch shell, light tan? It could've been recent. Within the last few days," I said.

Leslie scrunched her forehead. She opened the drawer under the cash register and pulled out a bundle of sales slips. "These are from the last few days," she said, flipping through them.

I reached for the familiar chewed pencil. Before I could bite down on it, I was interrupted by the noisy clamor of kids as they entered the store, their beach-chic dressed parents in tow. The middle-aged clerk sprang into action, her legs hurrying to assist a new family of tourists.

"Ah, here it is," Leslie exclaimed. She circled the

item and waved the sales slip. "I just sold this one recently."

I stopped mid-chew. My blood pulsed. "Could you do me a favor and tell me the name of the shell please?"

"Sure thing. Let me check our records and inventory list. I'd be happy to place an order for you," Leslie said.

"I came in earlier with Jake Thorne from the *Beach Beat* to buy a gift for my friend. But this time, I'm not here to buy. I'm following a lead on a story."

She met my eyes with raised eyebrows and dived into the paperwork.

Patience wasn't my virtue, but I'd learned to be better at it. I kept my expectations low while I waited.

"I found it," Leslie said. She was flushed with excitement. "We ordered a *Strombus latissimus,* and it was sold. It's the only one we had." She told me the date.

"A Strom ...?" I asked.

"Otherwise known as milk conch. This one was about six inches long."

My heartbeat quickened, my blood rushed, and my temple throbbed. Could this be the same conch found in Jeb's mouth? The description appeared to match.

"Do you remember who you sold it to? What he or she looked like?" I asked.

Leslie ran fingers through her hair. "It was a woman. I remember she had come in and asked for a large seashell. When I showed her this conch, she picked it up and said 'Oh, this is heavy.' I can't describe what she looked like, other than to say she wore sunglasses."

"Hmm," I said, chewing my pencil.

"And she had dark hair, pulled back in a ponytail."

"Would you happen to have a receipt?" I felt my hopes rising, but kept my voice calm.

Leslie went back to the drawer and pulled out the sales slip. She held it up, examining it. At that moment, I caught sight of the credit card receipt stapled on the back. I lurched forward, leaning closer to read the name. The half-chewed pencil was forgotten; it dropped from my lips, hurtling to the floor.

CHAPTER FORTY-SIX

I DASHED OUT OF THE STORE, HOLDING THE CELL PHONE to my ear as I waited for Jake to answer. When the call went to voice mail, I left a quick message about the *Strombus latissimus* and to please call me back pronto.

My mind raced with questions. Did Kaitlyn have anything to do with Jeb's murder? Was she involved with the plastics ban ordinance or corporate cover-ups? What, if any, was her relationship to Tony Moore? And the unthinkable—did Kaitlyn attack Blake and hire Moore to burglarize Cassie's place? Was Cassie still in danger? I headed toward home, bent on getting there as soon as possible.

I screeched to a halt in front of the beach house, but Cassie's car was gone. Bob's truck was still in the driveway. I jumped out of my car and ran up the driveway, charging into a surprised Bob.

"I'm sorry," I said, holding my hand up.

"Whoa," Bob said. "Slow down." He caught me and pulled me back.

I gasped, huffing to catch my breath.

"What's the big hurry?" he asked.

"Cassie, is she gone?"

"Yeah, she just left. What's going on?"

"I believe I know who was involved in Jeb's murder."

Bob sucked in his breath. His arms tightened around me.

"Okay take a deep breath, slow and easy," he said. "Now tell me what happened."

I told him about the seashell Kaitlyn had bought, the words tumbling out of my mouth. The timeline matched the day she was in town. That would explain the bit of hostility I sensed at the meeting in her office upon realizing I recognized her at the site of Blake's attack.

"Are you sure it was Kaitlyn?"

"I saw her name on the credit card receipt for the shell."

"Do you know for sure it was *the* shell found on the murdered person?"

"I'm getting it checked. I've put a call to Jake, and if I'm right, the shell will match the one the police have in possession. I believe the ladies in the store will attest to it. The *Strombus latissimus* was the only shell matching Jake's description in the store, and it was sold to Kaitlyn two days before Blake was attacked—the day she came into town."

Bob released his hold on me and rubbed his chin. "You've made quite a break in this case, Eve."

I nodded, my mind racing to tie up a few more loose ends. "That doesn't explain Kaitlyn's motive."

Silence settled between us. I was lost in thought, and from the look on his face, Bob was struggling to take all this in and make sense of it.

"Has there been any change to Blake's condition?" I asked, feeling guilty I hadn't gone to visit him again.

"He's still in a coma, but his condition has stabilized, and he may be improving. I know it hasn't gotten worse."

My cell phone jingled. It was Jake.

I mouthed to Bob, *Gotta take this call.*

"Jake, you got my message?" I didn't wait for him to speak and dived right in.

"I relayed your message to Perry. Wait until you hear the news."

"Can I put you on speakerphone? Bob's here with me," I said, my fingers ready to press the button.

"Go right ahead."

I tapped the speaker button.

"Hi, Bob."

"Hey, Jake, Eve filled me in. What's going on? Where are you?"

"I'm at the police station. Eve, you were absolutely right. The name you gave, *Strombus latissimus,* matched the identity of the seashell in their possession."

I gripped Bob's arm, and we locked eyes. "Kaitlyn."

"She is being taken in by the police now. They are on their way to her office as we speak."

"Did she hire the man in the suit?" I asked.

"Don't know yet. She'll be questioned about everything: the shell, Jeb's murder, the attack on Blake, the man in the suit."

"And the burglary of Cassie's beach house," Bob chimed in.

"Which reminds me," I said, turning to Bob. "Where did you say Cassie went?"

"I didn't say. She went to Nora's house."

CHAPTER FORTY-SEVEN

I WAS PRETTY GOOD AT MULTITASKING. IT CAME WITH lots of practice and necessity. Today was one of those days. I grabbed Bob and headed to my car.

"I know where Nora lives," I said. "Hang on Jake. Did you want to talk to Cassie again?"

"Yes, give me the address. I'll meet you there," he said.

In a small town, everything was close. I hadn't seen Nora since the first day I met her. It was only what, four or five days ago? But it felt longer.

On the way there, I stayed on the phone with Jake. I mentioned the time I met Nora on my first day at the beach. I hadn't gone back, and to my knowledge, Cassie hadn't, either. It had been a whirlwind of activity since I arrived. I knew how close the two of them were, and Cassie was the apple of Nora's eye.

We arrived almost simultaneously at Nora's house. Cassie's car was parked in front.

I beat Jake by about a minute, but I waited for him

to arrive to go in together. Bob had wanted to meet Nora since hearing us talk about her.

I'd texted Cassie, and she met us at the door. Nora was waiting inside in the living room. After introductions, we sat together on the couch.

Cassie had set a pitcher of iced tea and five glasses on the coffee table. We helped ourselves. It reminded me of the first time I sat with Nora on the porch and had iced tea.

We started talking at once, chatting like old friends and laughing, until Nora raised her hands up and hollered, "One at a time, please."

I told Nora what happened since I arrived, starting with the attack on Blake. Cassie, Jake, and Bob added to the story. Nora didn't interrupt. She sat and nodded every once in a while and asked questions. Maybe it was because we sat inside this time, but I thought her face looked worn out, and sensed a dreariness deep inside her. Maybe it was the shadows playing with my mind.

I watched and listened to the chatter. The excitement in the air was palpable. But something bugged me. A nagging thought, something still to be uncovered. I wished I had talked to Kaitlyn more. Something still didn't make sense. I put it away, for now. Kaitlyn was going to be interrogated.

CHAPTER FORTY-EIGHT

I DRIFTED IN AND OUT OF THE CONVERSATION. I BORED easily, and I'd heard all of it before already.

I looked around the room. I'd imagined a colorful, artsy interior with beach-themed decorations. The last time I was here, Cassie had gone in the house with Nora while I stayed outside. I'd been curious to see the inside. Her other house, where we were staying, had a youthful vibe. Here, it was more mature and less splashy.

"Right, Eve?"

I turned, realizing Cassie was asking me a question.

"What?"

"You solved the case."

"We all did," I said. I was sensing a strong vibe, and I knew when that happened, there was something going on.

"Would you like it back?" Nora was asking.

"Um, no," Cassie said.

My ears perked up. Did I miss something again?

"What is it?" I asked.

Cassie paused. "Oh, nothing, Blake asked me to keep something for him, and I left it here."

I sat up straight. This was the first time I'd heard of this.

I turned to Nora. "Why are you keeping Blake's stuff?"

"Cassie gave it to me," Nora said.

"When did you get it?"

"She brought it over the other day, you know, when you were here," Nora replied.

I had one of those lightbulb moments. My mind replayed the scene of my first visit. Cassie had gotten up to take Nora inside. I had followed, but in the doorway, Cassie had turned around and waved me off. I didn't go in.

"Brought what over, Nora?" I whispered.

"The thing young people use all the time."

"What thing?"

Out of the corner of my eye, Cassie had reached out to Nora.

"The stick, you know."

It didn't make any sense. I didn't see Cassie carry a stick that day. I shook my head. Maybe Nora was senile and making it all up?

"How long was the stick? What did it look like?" I asked.

Nora held her hand up, her fingers about two inches apart.

"It was purple. You stick it in the computer."

Now I understood. She was talking about a flash drive.

I looked at Cassie. Jake and Bob stared at me. It'd gotten quiet all of a sudden.

"Cassie, did you find anything missing after the burglary?"

"No," she said softly.

"Do you think the burglar was looking for the flash drive?"

She shrugged.

"When did Blake give it to you for safekeeping?"

"The night before we went to see Nora."

I was constructing the timeline in my head.

"So the night he called you, it was before nine in the evening, right?"

"Yes," Cassie said.

I chose my next words carefully.

"Blake is in a coma in the hospital. You've been burglarized. This flash drive may be what they were after and why Blake was attacked."

"What do we do now?" Bob asked.

Everyone spoke up at once. I held up my hand.

"I know it's Blake's, but he's in the hospital. What if it's the clue to solving his case?" I said.

A murmur went around the room. Someone said, "Blake's not here. We need to help him."

Cassie was quiet, though. "What if Blake doesn't want anyone to see it?"

"I know this is difficult to decide. If Blake was here

today, with us, we wouldn't be facing this situation—but he isn't," Jake said. He tapped his fingers on the table. Finally, he sighed and turned to Nora. "Can you bring us the stick please?"

CHAPTER FORTY-NINE

JAKE OPENED HIS SHOULDER BAG AND LIFTED OUT HIS laptop. I'd forgotten he carried his bag everywhere. Jake was ready, holding his hand out when Nora came back with the flash drive. I leaned over to look. The others crowded around.

There were two file folders in the drive. Jake opened the first, labeled "Blue Ocean." Inside were dozens of files. Corporate memorandums and internal emails, research studies with technical language, data, and graphs. A quick perusal gave the gist of it—the plastics industry had formulated a new plastic that was cheaper to produce and stronger, but the additives could be harmful, and it wasn't breakable using a new enzyme treatment being developed to treat plastics, adding to the garbage generated. It would affect the multimillion- or billion-dollar industries in production of plastics, which caused millions of tons of discarded plastic waste in the environment.

"Cassie, did Blake mention the contents in this flash drive?" Jake said.

"No, we didn't discuss it. He didn't tell me, and I didn't ask," Cassie said.

Jake turned to me. "Kaitlyn told us Blake wanted information. If she came down to give him these files, this proves she's telling the truth."

"It makes sense. Blake must have figured it contained important information or company secrets, and he put it on this flash drive to give to Cassie for safekeeping," I said. "I don't think Kaitlyn had anything to do with the burglary. Why would she, if she gave them to Blake?"

"We know Tony Moore has confessed to the burglary. Apparently, whoever is after this flash drive wanted it bad. My bet is people in the industry had a lot at stake—people with a lot to lose if this got out," Jake said.

Jake closed the folder and moved the cursor to the next one.

The second folder held a single file—a video.

CHAPTER FIFTY

MY EYES FIXED ON JAKE. MY FINGERS ITCHED TO PLAY the video. I had no idea what was on it or how long it was.

Jake leaned over his laptop. The room quickly silenced. Our eyes met for a moment before he clicked the touchpad to start the video.

The picture was inky dark. At first, I thought something was wrong with it. I couldn't see anything. I could hear the sound of the ocean, the waves surging and crashing on the shore. It was loud, but then my ears picked up faint human voices. I squinted, barely making out the two vague shapes moving—the silhouettes of a man and a woman, at first standing apart, then coming together to embrace before the shapes flattened on the beach. I strained to listen and see.

A sliver of moonlight beamed, moving from behind the clouds. A closer shot. Blake lying on the beach naked, sand tangled in his locks of sandy brown hair, his face upturned, his mouth parted. A woman hovered over him, her long, dark hair swept by the wind, her slim, bare back arching and swaying. The crashing of waves could not mute their loud cries, first the woman's and then the man joining her, crescendoing to an euphoric high.

Afterwards, a shout. "Who's there?" The picture shook, and the frame shifted and flickered, swinging widely and catching sight of an orange fabric and the tip of a shoe before it veered down to the ground, and images of a shoreline whizzed by, punctuated by the heavy panting of someone running.

It ended abruptly.

EPILOGUE

I WOULD NEVER FORGET THAT SUMMER AT LOLLY BEACH. I thought I was grown-up, but I was wrong. Life wasn't something you could always plan. It finds you, throws you in a loop, and leaves you to live it out, for better or worse.

Jake and I kept in touch. He wrote the story and gave me credit on the byline in *Beach Beat*, which was picked up by national newspapers and won an award. The plastics ban ordinance did pass, although by a narrow margin. The estimated cost would eventually be offset by the increased revenue from tourism with the promotion of their family-friendly, clean beach. Jake enjoyed the thrill of a good story, and there was plenty more to write. It ran in his blood. He was offered a promotion to editor, but Jake stayed doing what he loved the most—being a veteran reporter.

As for Kaitlyn, she was doing time for Jeb's murder. She was in love with Blake, her adopted sibling. She'd even checked on marriage. They weren't related by blood, and marriage wasn't illegal. Their union wouldn't be messing up the gene pool. But Blake had struggled with the ethics of it, and they had a falling out after college. Kaitlyn's feelings for Blake roared back up when they met again. Under the moonlight, she released her pent-up sexual longing and—in a moment of crazed frenzy—Blake let down his guard and caved in to the powerful urges. Jeb had watched and filmed them from afar, but when he moved in for a close-up, he was discovered. Kaitlyn was outraged.

A few days later, she had followed Jeb, wearing an orange T-shirt, to the beach and confronted him about the secret taping. In his naiveté and confusion, Jeb blurted out the name of the lucky lady who inspired Blake's special crêpe. It *wasn't* Kaitlyn. They struggled. He fell, his head striking a sharp rock. In a fit of livid rage, she had reached in her purse, grabbed the *Strombus latissimus* and pummeled the cracked head of the dying man, before ramming it in Jeb's mouth, sealing forever the lips that had just revealed the cruel truth. After Jeb died, Kaitlyn took his cell phone and threw it in the ocean, but she didn't know Jeb had already made a copy of the video and gave it to Blake.

Tony Moore ultimately confessed to attacking Blake, in addition to the burglary. He had followed Blake and watched him give the flash drive to Cassie. He still insisted he never knew who hired him or made the surreptitious arrangements. The police put a freeze on his bank account and looked for links or ties to plastic corporations. But a search of his premises didn't turn up any evidence.

Blake was released from the hospital. Doctors had told him it would be a long journey ahead. Some lucky people recovered before long and went on with their lives as normally as possible. For others, like Blake, the prognosis was uncertain. It could take months or years or decades. He'd have to continue with his treatments and deal with the excruciating pain in his head, nausea, sleep disturbance, ringing in his ears, and a multitude of other symptoms, which would affect his quality of life and ability to function. Blake had an unshakable will to survive, and he was determined to get better.

Cassie stayed at the beach the rest of the summer—and took a leave of absence from school in the fall. Her father was furious and threatened to disown her. But Cassie was stubborn and didn't want his money. She took care of Nora. When it was her time to pass on, Cassie was by her side as Nora took her last breath. She remained a steady friend to Blake. Their romantic relationship blossomed. The last time I heard from Cassie was her letter inviting me to their engagement party.

And, oh … I would never look at a peach the same way again. Blake did finally make crêpes for me. He named his special creation *"The Cassandra."* I had never tasted crêpes that good, nor would I ever again.

And I did make it to the oyster bar. On my last day at Lolly Beach, they took me there—Cassie, Blake, Nora, Jake, Larry, Bob, and even Mrs. Berry and her husband. I ordered a huge plate of oysters in the shell.

It took me longer to shuck them than to eat them, and boy, did I cuss. Did I tell you how much work it was? In the end, it was worth it. I slurped the delicious, fresh oysters, filling my belly until I could no more. We laughed and ate. I had so much fun.

BOOKS BY JANE SUEN

Children of the Future

EVE SAWYER MYSTERIES

Murder Creek

Murder at Lolly Beach

FLOWERS IN DECEMBER TRILOGY

Flowers in December

Coming Home

Second Chance

ALTERATIONS TRILOGY

Alterations

Game Changer

Primal Will

SHORT STORIES

Beginnings and Endings: A Selection of Short Stories

Made in the USA
Columbia, SC
01 February 2023